力得文化
Leader Culture

Lead your way, be your own leader!

力得文化
Leader Culture

Lead your way, be your own leader!

CHARMING & GLOWING:
COMMUNICATIONS IN MARKETING, ADVERTISING, AND PR

力得文化
Leader Culture

行銷公關英語
超有料

超越行銷公關 **有料**才是王道
提升**英語能力** 打造專業形象

46% ENGLISH COMMUNICATION SKILLS
語言能力

42% GOOD-LOOKING
外表

35% KNOWLEDGEABLE
內涵

31% DIPLOMATIC
手腕

28% TASTEFUL 品味

18% AMBITIOUS 企圖心

江昀璟、胥淑嵐 ◎著

附MP3

本書特色

25個實用主題:
資深行銷公關執筆
=真實歷練+職場百態

50篇情境對話:
專業外籍配音員錄製MP3
=聽說合一 效率學習

【主題對話】與主管、客戶開會、
簡報、媒體採購、主視覺拍攝
=正式溝通 精彩有料

【延伸對話】與同事、外製閒聊哈啦
=非正式溝通 關鍵加分

【有料字彙+句型】捨棄繁複文法分
析+不囉嗦直接給例句
=現學現用 立刻上手

行銷/公關/廣告人 有料必備!
加薪/升職/跳槽 捨我其誰!

作者序
Preface

　　擔任公關的職場生涯中，曾經遇過各式各樣大小的突發狀況，以及各種類型的活動，公關的角色確實相當不容易，除了面面俱到，又得因應法規、人情、媒體、消費者、公司主管等多方的壓力，一路走來，很希望有機會能將所歷練過的經驗，能夠分享給剛剛進入公關領域的人，讓後進能借由這本書，從中得到許多平日字典裡查不到，且真實職場上常用的英文敘述，用簡單的對話，一一清楚地呈現出在大型外商企業環境中，各自角色的扮演，以及職責分擔，內文中所有的對話情節，皆非杜撰，都是真實發生過的案例，也可供給大家日後在處理相關的事件上，多一些考慮與參考的方向。

江昀璟

　　公關界流行一句話：「公關就是企業的最佳化妝師！」由此可見，公關對企業的重要不言可喻。而行銷，是影響人們生活的至要商業活動；消費者的許多購買決策，殊不知其實是受了行銷人員的左右。

　　本書將行銷與公關行業常見的實務場景，以國際語言─英語撰寫而成，相信可以幫助許多正在，或者是想要踏入這個行業的讀者，增進相關的英語實力。

胥淑嵐

編者序
Words from Editor

　　你有外表、有內涵，還有手腕。你的企圖心旺盛也拼勁十足。但長期熬夜和壓力讓你沒健康也沒朋友？永遠在幫客戶危機處理，你看見自己的危機嗎？無時無刻不想加薪，想跳槽，但這一行大家不都是這樣優秀又這樣肯拼，你又憑什麼？

　　為客戶解決問題，更要為自己創造價值。既然聰明的你懂得如何用三萬塊的預算幫客戶做出五萬塊的質感，更應該知道要利用甚至創造各種機會來加強自己優勢的重要。

　　在專業能力之外，語言能力的提升被視為職場競爭力的關鍵。《行銷公關英語超有料》的對話，選自 25 個行銷公關常見主題情境，有正式的【主題會話】（開會、簡報），也有非正式的【延伸對話】（茶水間、午飯時間），給您「英語環境」。沒有艱澀的文法解說，有的是實用好用的【有料句型】與【短句補給】，讓您「效率學習」。

　　用體力、腦力得到主管、客戶認同的同時也該有所累積。人前保持光鮮亮麗的外表，人後期許自己內在更有料。現在就跟著《行銷公關英語超有料》一起提升職場語言力，共同打造屬於你的個人品牌!

倍斯特編輯部

目次
Contents

3. 媒體採購／Media Buy

行銷是創造、溝通與傳送價值給客戶的一連串活動；這些活動包含開始的策略擬定、市場劃分，到產品的研發、塑型、定價，以及通路的選擇、促銷活動的內容…等等，包羅萬象。

1.
行銷
Marketing

The initial meeting of the 2016 marketing strategy planning will be conducted on next Monday. I am worried about how to prepare myself. According to senior colleagues, we will be holding a series of these meetings in the upcoming weeks. The topics like core marketing strategy, promotion calendar, overall budget, and communication theme will all be covered.

下週一將召開第一次的年度行銷策略會議，我要從哪裡開始準備呢？聽資深的同事表示，這樣的會議將在幾週內密集進行好幾次，包括整年度所有的行銷策略、活動行事曆、預算和溝通主題，全部都會被討論到。

Dialogue 1　主題對話

Where Shall I Begin? 該從哪開始？

情境說明 Situation

During the preparation of the 2016 marketing strategy planning, everyone on the marketing team is required to submit the final presentation power point slides for the secretary's consolidation by the end of the week. The marketing manager now is dispatching the preparation assignments of the presentation slides.

在年度行銷會議準備期間，每一位行銷部同仁都要在本週之內提交簡報的最後版本檔案給秘書，讓秘書將所有的檔案進行整合。目前行銷經理正在分配同仁們各自應準備的簡報內容。

情境對話 Dialogue

Manager: Tom, please prepare the topic of "Summer Fever Party" since you are the project owner.

經理：湯姆，由於「夏日狂熱派對」的產品是由你負責上市，因此請你準備這個主題的資料。

Tom: Noted. How many pages would be enough?

Tom：請問需要幾頁的簡報？

Manager: We have 90 minutes in total for five topics, including four quarters and year-end promotion, so 10 slides for one topic would be appropriate. Usually one slide would take around 2 minutes, and we need to leave some time for answering questions.

經理：我們整體報告的時間為一個半小時，需要帶到五個主題，包含四個季節主題與年終特賣，因此每個主題約十張簡報即可。通常一張簡報的說明大約為兩分鐘，我們還需要預留一點時間讓大家提問，並予以説明。

Tom: I see. I will use one slide to cover strategy. And I will briefly cover the 6Ps like product, people, place, promotion, price and profit. But I am not sure how to present the place and forecast the profit.

Tom：了解，那麼我會用一頁的簡報說明主題策略，並以 6P 的分類說明產品、銷售業代（或營運人員）、銷售地點、促銷方式、新品價格與利潤。但是，我不確定要如何呈現銷售地點這部分與利潤預測。

Manager: The place, it could be introduced by 2 parts. The first part would be the launch event venue and décor. Secondly, you could present the in-store POSMs during the whole campaign period.

經理：關於銷售地點，可以呈現主要兩部分。第一部分為上市活動地點與佈置主題，另一部份為活動期間的銷售店家製作物有哪些。

Tom: Right. What about the profit?

Tom：好的，那麼在利潤的部分呢？

Manager: There are two ways to do projection -- previous showcase or competitor learning.

經理：也是兩個部分，從過去成功的上市經驗與競爭品牌的案例，來做你的預估。

Tom: For this project, what is your advice?

Tom：那麼這次的案子，您的建議是？

Manager: Although there was no identical Summer Party showcase done previously that we could check, still there was a similar summer promotion done in 2011. I suggest you take a look at it.

經理：雖然過去上市的經驗中，從未操作過完全一樣「夏日派對」的主題，不過在 2011 年有一個夏季促銷的活動，是一個可以參考案例。

Tom: I will consider the sales numbers from 2011 and add a bit to it. As back in 2011, we only had 11 stores, but currently we have 20 stores, so the sales base nowadays is much bigger.

Manager: Good point. But just as a reminder, don't be too aggressive about the projection. The economy is on a downturn compared to 2011, and our sales numbers compared to the same time in 2011 has declined.

Tom: Do we have to mention media plan?

Manager: No need to go into details due to our limit on time. Just briefly mentioning how to approach it would be ok.

Tom: Where can I obtain the gross profit margin of each product?

Manager: You can ask Finance department to provide you the information.

Tom: Any other remarks?

Manager: Not really, but maybe you could post a chart of the campaign timeline and total cost of this project.

Tom：我會參考 2011 的銷售數字之後，再增加一些。因為在 2011 年時，我們的銷售店家只有 11 家，而目前我們已經擁有 20 家店，銷售的基本量較往年大了許多。

經理：很好的角度。但是我也提醒你，預估數字別過度樂觀，因為時下經濟與市場較 2011 年時衰退，我們今年度的同期銷售數字較 2011 還低。

Tom：我們需要提到媒體計劃嗎？

經理：因為說明的時間不多，所以不需要寫到細節，只要提出會採用那些媒體即可。

Tom：請問我在哪裡可以取得每一樣產品的毛利率？

經理：你可以去找財務部，他們會提供這樣的資訊。

Tom：還有其他要注意的嗎？

經理：都還好。不過也許你可以加一個活動時程表，以及這個案子預算總額。

ABC 有料字彙 *Vocabulary*

- **upcoming** (*n.*) [`ʌp͵kʌmɪŋ] 即將到來
  The company's **upcoming** product will benefit future investment.
  這家公司的新產品將有助於未來投資。

- **consolidation** (*n.*) [kən͵salə`deʃən] 整合，強化
  When it goes to **consolidation**, it has something to do with jointing and combining.
  當談到 consolidation 這個詞彙，就跟「聯合」與「結合」有關。

- **assignment** (*n.*) [ə`saɪnmənt] 任務，（被分派的）工作
  It was more than an **assignment** to host a party for that company.
  幫那家公司主持派對可不只是個工作而已（更別具意義）。

- **POSM** Point of Sales Material 銷售地點的廣告促銷物
  POSM is the advertising materials that are used to communicate brand information to the consumers, including streamers and posters.
  POSM 指的是用來溝通品牌訊息的廣告材料，包括有橫幅長旗跟海報。

- **showcase** (*n.*) [ʃo͵kes] 具優點或代表性的東西
  The exhebition was a **showcase** for young artists.
  這展覽是年輕藝術家展現才華的地方。

- **identical** (*a.*) [aɪ`dɛntɪk!] 完全一樣的
  These two ideas may be alike, but not **identical**.
  這兩個想法或許很像，但並不完全一樣。

- **nowadays** (*adv.*) [`naʊə͵dez] 現今，時下
  Office workers **nowadays** are under a lot more stress than ever.
  現今的上班族比以往承擔了更多的壓力。

- **downturn** (*n.*) [`daʊntɝn] 經濟衰退
  The **downturn** has presented a nice entry point for investors.
  經濟衰退提供了投資者一個絕佳的進場時機。

- **profit margin** 利潤率，毛利率
  Profit margin can be thought as the amount of profit that a company keeps per dollar of revenue.
  毛利率可以被想做是一家公司每一塊錢的收入所賺的利潤。

- **timeline** (*n.*) [taɪmlaɪn] 時間表，時程表
  It will be easier to memorize if you write out a **timeline** when you study the brand history.
  當你在研究品牌歷史時，（依先後順序）畫出時間線來，會比較容易記得住。

🐤🐤 **有料句型** Sentence Pattern

句型 1 ↘

I suggest you to ...　我建議你…。

I suggest you to have a look at it.
我建議你看看這個。

I suggest you to bring the book back.
我建議你將書帶回來。

I suggest them to cook dinner at home.
我建議他們在家煮晚餐。

句型 2 ↘

Although..., still... 雖然…，卻還是…。

Although there was no showcase, **still** there was a similar case could be check.

雖然沒有案例，但還是有個相似的案子可以參考。

Although he is ill, **still** he wants to go to work.

雖然他生病了，但是還是想去上班。

Although she has many shoes, **still** she would love to shop more.

她雖然已經有很多鞋子，卻仍然還是想買。

句型 3 ↘

go into details 進入細節

We should **go into details** today.

我們今天應該談談細節。

Let's **go into details**!

讓我們來討論細節吧!

I don't think we have time to **go into details**.

我不認為我們有時間談細節。

Expert Tips
知識補給

Generally speaking, the marketing strategy meetings will be conducted during the second half of the year, before the year-end. Such meetings are intensively held several times in weeks. Those yearly marketing strategies won't be submitted to the headquarters until they go through several revisions, discussions, and confirmations. The strategies include quarterly marketing strategies, total budget and communication theme. Each strategy, promotion, and theme are required to fit the overall company policy and direction. For example, if the company overall direction of the year is "Youth and Innovation," then "being young and innovative" is supposed to be checked all the time in all the marketing activities and strategies.

　　一般來說，每一年年底前，都會進行下年度的行銷策略會議，這樣的會議通常在幾週內密集進行好幾次，最後幾經修改、討論、確認後，年度行銷策略才會提交到總部，包括每一季主要的行銷策略、預算總額和溝通主題，無須寫到太細節的執行內容，但是每一個主要行銷策略、與活動促銷與溝通方向，都也需要符合公司整體策略與方向，比如說：如公司年度整體方向為「年輕化與創新」，則所有的行銷活動與策略上，要時時檢視是否符合年輕化與創新的方向。

Dialogue 2　延伸對話

Get Started the Sooner the Better 越早開始越好

情境說明 *Situation*

Steve and Richard are colleagues in the Marketing Department, and they are working on their own projects recently.　One day, they happen to meet each other at staff room.

史帝夫和李察是行銷部門的同事，最近他們忙於各自的專案。有一天，他們碰巧在茶水間遇到了。

♀♂角色介紹 *Characters*

Steve: Responsible for promotion event planning.
Richard: Responsible for public relations.

史帝夫：負責促銷活動規劃。
李察：負責公共關係。

💬 情境對話 *Dialogue*

Steve: Hey, Richard.　What have you been up to lately?

史帝夫：嘿，李察。最近在忙些什麼？

Richard: Hi, Steve.　Nothing special, you?

李察：嗨，史帝夫。沒什麼特別的事情，你呢？

Steve: I am doing quite well, but I heard that you are facing many questions that are still remaining unanswered.

史帝夫：還不錯啦，但是我聽說你正面臨一些懸而未決的事情呢。

Richard: <u>Well, what else I can say?</u> It seems that delay creating an annual marketing plan is already became our Department's unquitable bad habit.

李察：呃，我還能説什麼？看來延遲提出年度行銷計畫，已經成了我們部門戒不掉的壞習慣了。

Steve: <u>Well saying!</u> I hate that, too.

史帝夫：説得好！我也很討厭這樣。

Richard: Personally, I just think we should start making any plan half year ago. Then I will have more time to come out a better annual PR plan.

李察：個人意見啦，我只是覺得我們應該提早半年就開始企畫。我才會有更多時間提出一個好的年度公關計畫。

Steve: Indeed, the annual marketing plan is everything we follow.

史帝夫：確實，年度行銷計畫是我們跟隨的依據。

Richard: I guess we have to tell our Boss together.

李察：我想我們應該一起去找主管談談。

Steve: Well, you could try it but <u>don't hold your breath.</u>

史帝夫：嗯，這個嘛，你可以試啦，但是別抱太大期望。

短句補給 Useful Phrases

✓ Well, what else I can say? 呃，我還能説什麼呢？
✓ Well saying! 説的好！
✓ Don't hold your breath. 別抱太大期望了。

市場與競爭品牌分析
1-2 Market Analysis

A chance to plan the launch of a brand from start to finish is always exciting. The market analysis comprehends full perspectives such as market scale, market share, product segmentation, potential barriers, product life cycle, and the SWOT to come up with a final analysis. After this step, we would have further brainstorming discussion about strategies.

能夠有機會參與一個全新品牌的上市，總是讓人非常興奮。市場分析通常會用一個完整的角度去了解市場需求大小、市占率、產品分階、預期挑戰、產品週期以及優劣點，當全盤了解後，就會進行討論來決定策略。

1 行銷

2 廣告

3 媒體採購

4 公關公司

5 網路行銷

6 企業社會形象

Dialogue 1　主題對話　03

I'll Try to Use Some Connections to Gather All of That!
我會試著透過關係收集那些的!

 情境說明 *Situation*

Today, we are having a briefing with the advertising agency for a new brand launch to a market. The brand would be introduced to the public 10 months later. We would like to have a complete market analysis.

我們今天正在和廣告公司進行一個新品牌上市的發包簡報,這個品牌將在十個月後上市。我們需要一個完整的市場分析。

情境對話 *Dialogue*

Marketing Manager: This is a brand that was founded in US in 1950. The iconic product of this brand will be introduced to the Taiwan market in October; however, it is not the local production. So our pricing cannot be compatible and production delivery is not controllable.

Agency: The brand is already well known and very familiar to local consumers. The market is full of locally made copycats. "Original and Imported" could be its

行銷經理:這個品牌是 1950 年於美國創立。今年十月,台灣的消費者將會見到這個品牌旗下最具代表性的產品。然而,由於產品並非本地製造,因此價位上是無法有競爭力,並且製程運送的時間較無法掌握。

廣告公司:這個品牌已經是很有知名度,而本地消費者也很熟悉。市場上有很多本地製造的雷同產品,因此強

uniqueness and key success factor as well as a unique selling point.

Marketing Manager: I need to know how many similar products have been sold in the past three years, including which brands (competitors), the product portfolios of those brands, and price segmentation.

Agency: No problem. I will incorporate all of this into the analysis.

Marketing Manager: Concerning the competitors, I hope you can obtain the intelligence of their brand positioning, monthly sales, production, promotion, channel development, media spending, and market share.

Agency: That would be slightly difficult. I will try to use some connections to gather all of that.

Marketing Manager: I heard that one of the competitors is sponsoring a musical program. Do you have further information on that?

Agency: Yes, I do have it. Brand X started to do the sponsorship 3 years ago, and it did help significantly to enhance the brand impression and target consumer's

調『原創品牌與原裝進口』會是很有利的關鍵成功因素。

行銷經理：我需要了解市場上在過去幾年間，共有多少雷同產品、哪些競爭品牌、這些牌子有哪些產品線、價位分級為何？

廣告公司：我會集結這些資料在分析報告內。

行銷經理：關於競爭品牌，我希望你可以取得對方的品牌定位、業績月報、製造與促銷、通路開發、媒體採購花費和市占率等上述相關的情報。

廣告公司：這會有點難度。不過我會儘量透過關係來收集。

行銷經理：我聽說某個競爭品牌正在贊助音樂表演，你有相關的資料嗎？

廣告公司：我剛好手邊有，這個X品牌從三年前開始贊助活動，這活動確實幫品牌加了分，並且也得到很多目

attention.

Marketing Manager: Right. Please let me know their sponsorship budget scale and outcome over the past years.

Agency: Noted.

Marketing Manager: Do you think the economic downturn will affect the industry?

Agency: Not quite. Despite the environment change, many people still intent to own some quality-worthy and branded products.

Marketing Manager: We plan to launch this brand with its iconic product to test the water. Once we evaluate the public reaction and acceptance toward it, and we could launch its serial models in the future if more opportunities appear.

Agency: If so, I think we need to look into the numbers of potential growth and product life cycle assessment.

Marketing Manager: Indeed.

Agency: When would we have our brainstorming discussion?

Marketing Manager: Can I say 5 days from today?

Agency: Great! I will get everything prepared.

標消費群的注意。

行銷經理：對，請給我過去幾年來他們贊助的總金額。

廣告公司：好的。

行銷經理：你認為目前的經濟衰退會不會對市場有影響？

廣告公司：應該還好。雖然環境有些改變，但是多數的人仍傾向要擁有品質好、具品牌的產品。

行銷經理：我們計劃先上市這個品牌旗下最具代表性的產品來試水溫，評估一下市場反應及接受度。如果有機會的話，未來我們也會上市一系列的產品。

廣告公司：如果是這樣，我想我們需要了解一下市場成長潛力與產品週期。

行銷經理：沒錯。

廣告公司：我們什麼時候進行腦力激盪討論？

行銷經理：我想建議五天後？

廣告公司：好的，我會將一切準備好。

ABC 有料字彙 Vocabulary

- **comprehend** (v.) [ˌkɑmprɪˋhɛnd] 包含，包括
  Some prices in the samples **comprehend** transportation costs.
  有些樣品的價格包含了運送成本。

- **segmentation** (n.) [ˌsɛɡmənˋteʃən] 區隔
  This market **segmentation** can attract more target customers to the brand.
  這個市場區隔能為品牌吸引更多目標顧客。

- **brainstorm** (v.) [brenˌstɔrm] 集體討論，集思廣益
  Brainstorming is a process for generating ideas through group discussions.
  腦力激盪是指透過團體討論來發想的過程。

- **iconic** (a.) [aɪˋkɑnɪk] 代表性的
  Captain America is recognizable by his **iconic** shield and dramatic muscle.
  美國隊長藉由他那具有代表性的盾牌與戲劇化的肌肉而具識別度。

- **copycat** (n.) [ˋkɑpɪˌkæt] 抄襲者，模仿者
  Good design attracts attention and also leads to **copycat** products.
  好設計引人注意也會有抄襲者。

- **portfolio** (n.) [portˋfolɪˌo] 組合，目錄
  To impress your future boss, you can present a **portfolio** of your best works.
  要讓你未來的老闆驚豔，你可以將你最好的作品組合呈現。

- **incorporate** (v.) [ɪnˋkɔrpəˌret] 合併，整合
  The product design **incorporates** wooden and metal structures

to create a sense of conflict.

這項產品設計整合了木頭和金屬的結構來產生一種衝突感。

- **intelligence** (*n.*) [ɪnˋtɛlədʒəns] 情報，消息
One of the emphases at the meeting was on how to gather useful **intelligence** about the rivals.

這會議其中一個重點就是如何蒐集對手有用情報。

- **to test the water** （市場）試水溫
We will provide 5,000 free giveaways **to test the water**.

我們會提供 5,000 份免費贈品先試個水溫。

- **indeed** (*adv.*) [ɪnˋdid] 當然，確實
Indeed, photos and footage of food, pets, and babies are real eye-catchers.

確實，食物、寵物和嬰兒的照片和影片最吸睛。

🐦🐦 **有料句型** *Sentence Pattern*

句型 1 ↘

... is well + p.p. …是（被）…的。

The brand **is well known.**
這牌子廣為人知（被人熟知）。

The dog **is well trained**.
那隻狗（被）訓練有素。

She **is well dressed**.
她是精心打扮過。

句型 2 ↘

Despite..., still... 儘管…，還是…。

Despite the environment change, many people **still** intent to own it.
儘管環境改變，許多人仍想要擁有它。

Despite his illness, **still** he decided to go to work today.
儘管他有病在身，今天仍然決定去上班。

Despite the price, **still** I will buy the product.
不論價格如何，我還是會買這產品。

句型 3 ↘

n. -worthy 值得…的；在…方面有好評價的

That is a **quality-worthy** product.
這是一項有好品質的產品。

I need a **price-worthy** car.
我需要一部值得這個價格的車。

He is a **trustworthy** person.
他是個值得信賴的人。

Expert Tips
知識補給

The marketing analysis is a constant research. Before pricing and positioning are not established yet, the analysis usually targets at leading brands, focusing on current market trend, need, and sales figures to evaluate the pricing policy and to forecast the sales volume. Once you establish your own brand pricing and positioning, the analysis goes to those brands which has real impact with your own brand. During this period, the marketing strategies, products, services, and how the PR functions are emphasized.

市場與競爭品牌分析是一種會持續進行的研究，當自己的品牌定價與定位尚未確認前，競爭品牌分析通常以市場主要的領導品牌為主，會著重在市場現況、市場需求、銷售數字以評估定價策略與業績預測；一旦當自己的品牌定價與定位確認後，則會針對與自己品牌具有實際影響力的競爭品牌進行研究，此時會比較著重在對方的行銷策略、產品力、服務內容、公關運作。

Dialogue 2　延伸對話

Keep Your Eyes on the Competitors 緊盯你的對手

情境說明 *Situation*

Anna works under Bill's management, and they are discussing the competitive analysis of the new cosmetic products which are going to be launched.

比爾是安娜的上司，他們正在討論即將新推出的彩妝用品的市場競爭分析。

♀♂角色介紹 *Characters*

Bill: Marketing Manager
Anna: Marketing Specialist

比爾：行銷部經理
安娜：行銷部專員

情境對話 *Dialogue*

Bill: I need you to make some corrections on this report.

比爾：安娜，我需要妳修改一下這份報告。

Anna: <u>I would love to</u>, but, I am not sure which part I should make the adjustment.

安娜：我很願意，但是，我不曉得應該加強哪一個部分？

Bill: The upcoming cosmetics mainly focus on the feature of dark spot correcting.

比爾：即將上市的彩妝用品強調遮瑕功能。但是這裡的

1 行銷

2 廣告

3 媒體採購

4 公關公司

5 網路行銷

6 企業社會形象

However, the competitor brands here are all with feature of ...

競爭品牌特色都是帶…

Anna: OK, I think I get the point now.

安娜：好的，我想我懂了。

Bill: Moreover, there are more and more Korean brands on the market now, we should keep our eyes on them.

比爾：還有，韓國品牌在市場上也逐漸多起來，我們應該緊盯著這些品牌。

Anna: But our brand is an American brand.

安娜：但是我們是美系的。

Bill: It doesn't matter. We could use this opportunity to understand if the customers take "nationality" into consideration when they buy cosmetics.

比爾：沒有關係。正好藉此了解一下目標消費者，購買時是否會考慮是哪一個國家的化妝品。

Anna: I see.

安娜：我懂了。

Bill: You can finish it by tomorrow noon, can't you?

比爾：明天中午以前可以完成吧？

Anna: I guess yes, Boss.

安娜：應該可以，老闆。

短句補給 Useful Phrases

✓ I would love to. 我很願意。
✓ I think I get the point now. 我想我懂了。
✓ Keep our eyes on them. 緊盯著對方。

Who are our consumers? Where are they? How can we attract them to purchase our products? The more we understand our consumers, the easier it will be to position the brand and employ the best strategy for selling the product.

誰是我們的消費者？他們在哪裡？如何才能吸引他們來購買產品？要更了解潛在的消費者，才能更容易去定位品牌與設定策略，讓產品大賣。

1 行銷

2 廣告

3 媒體採購

4 公關公司

5 網路行銷

6 企業社會形象

Dialogue 1　主題對話

Find Your Potential Customers! 找出你的潛在客戶群！

 情境說明 *Situation*

Prior to a product or brand launch, a concept test or market survey will be conducted to estimate the market potential, find out the consumer profile for the product and test the preference of the communication concept. Today the survey result has been received. The team is discussing the result.

在一個產品上市之前，針對了目標消費群進行分析，找出市場潛力、可能來消費的群眾輪廓，還有群眾偏好方向。今天分析報告已經出來，市調公司與行銷團隊正在討論該分析報告的內容。

情境對話 *Dialogue*

Agency: According to the preliminary research result, the data indicates that the target might scatter across a very wide range. It could very well turn out not to be a single group with a similar demographic background. Therefore, we randomly picked those who really want to buy the vehicle as a whole, analyzed who they are, and followed up with a summary of the picture of the main target. A total of two surveys are to be delivered, firstly,

市調公司：在最初的調查的階段，我們發現，結果會因為地理區域的不同而很分散，很有可能會導致沒有一個組別，彼此會有類似的區域背景。因此我們決定隨機挑出想要一群全都正要買車的群眾，以這群眾為主體，再加以分析他們的背景，因此出現主要潛在消費者的輪廓。我們總共安排了兩場主

Communication Concept Test and Target Profile Audit: This is to find out the characteristics of the target group as well as the way, and the content they prefer. Secondly, **Market Potential Study**: This is to test a wide age range in the current 1,600cc and up vehicle user group, in order to find the TA with market potential.

Manager: What is the sample size?
Agency: 200 people for survey one and 500 for survey two, Taiwan island-wide.

Manager: Good. Please proceed.
Agency: In the survey, respondents showed a higher purchase intention toward the 1,500cc XXX brand or OOO brand with a sales price between NT$ 1,120,000 and 1,800,000. The intention is determined by a 10-point scale with the score higher than 7(or equal). Among them, 60% are male while 40% are female. Plus, we found out that those who are currently using 1,600cc or above vehicles are between ages 25 and 50.

Manager: How about the color preference?

要的調查，第一波為「概念測試與背景調查」，這主要是找出潛在消費者的個性特質，以及他們喜歡的內容。第二波則是「市場潛力調查」，這部分則是找出不分年齡之目前 1,600cc 以上的汽車車主，來看出未來市場需求。

經理：請問測試人次為何？

市調公司：第一波為 200 人，而第二波為 500 人，以台灣本島為主。

經理：好，請繼續說明。

市調公司：在測試中，回應者顯示出對於 1,500cc 以上不論 XXX 牌或 OOO 牌的高購買意願，只要價位介於新台幣 112 萬至 180 萬之間，意願比以一至十分為評等，而這個價位的購買意願落在七或高於七。在全部受訪者中，男性占百分之六十，女性則為四十。我們發現那些目前開 1,600cc 或以上的車主的年齡介於 25 至 50 之間。

經理：請問顏色的喜好？

1 行銷

2 廣告

3 媒體採購

4 公關公司

5 網路行銷

6 企業社會形象

Agency: The Gentleman Blue is most preferred, by both male and female.

Manager: Then we have to order more of that color and also consider listing the Gentleman Blue at a higher price. What are the top five reasons that lead consumers to refuse to buy this new model? Also, what are the top five important factors that would incline them to make a purchase? What are their education and job background, likely character and personality?

Agency: I will send you the file with the full analyse of the whole survey. Regarding their background and likely character, I will share with you the file later when discussing Brand Positioning and Strategy next week.

Manager: How about the communication concept test; we have the two "Classic & Tradition" and "Modern & Trendy" themes, but which one gets more points?

Agency: "Modern & Trendy" won more votes.

Manager: That's difficult. Since our key

市調公司：「紳士藍」是最受歡迎的顏色，不分性別。

經理：那麼我們必須訂多一些紳士藍的存量，且也考慮讓這個顏色的價位較其他顏色高一些。哪些是前五名原因消費者不願購買這款新產品？ 哪些又是他們考慮願意購買的前五項因素？ 他們的教育與工作背景是如何？ 個性與品格特質又是哪些？

市調公司：我會寄給你一個前五大排名願意購買與不願購買的原因分析，關於這些潛在消費者的背景與性格特質等等，我在下週品牌定位與策略的會議中會提出。

經理：那麼請問一下概念測試的結果如何？ 在傳播溝通製作物的風格設計，我們有兩種風格，一種是「傳統與經典」另一種是「時尚與流行」？

市調公司：較多人選擇喜歡「時尚與流行」的風格設計。

經理：這就有點難度。畢竟

success factor and unique selling point is
"Origin and Imported", that seems to suit
"Classic & Tradition" better.

我們關鍵成功因素是原創與
原裝，這一點是比較容易與
「傳統與經典」來結合的。

ABC 有料字彙 Vocabulary

- **employ** (v.) [ɪm`plɔɪ] 利用，使用
  Computers **employing** the latest microprocessors have been their
  flagship products.
  載有最新微處理器的電腦是他們的主打商品。

- **potential** (a.) [pə`tɛnʃəl] 可能的，潛在的
  We try to reach our **potential** customers by the market survey.
  我們試著用市場調查來找出潛在客戶。

- **preliminary** (a.) [prɪ`lɪmə,nɛrɪ] 預先的，初步的
  The data and conclusions should be viewed in a **preliminary**
  stage.
  在最初階段，應先仔細審閱資料和結論。

- **scatter** (v.) [`skætɚ] 分散，零落
  It's been very **scattered** for people to get clear information.
  消息很分散，人們難以得到明確資訊。

- **demographic** (a.) [ˌdimə`græfɪk] 人口統計分佈
  We target at the 30-40 year old **demographic** background due to
  their spending power.
  我們瞄準 30 到 40 歲的年齡層是因為這年齡層的消費力。

- **randomly** (adv.) [`rændəmlɪ] 任意的，隨機的

1 行銷
2 廣告
3 媒體採購
4 公關公司
5 網路行銷
6 企業社會形象

Don't just give those samples **randomly**.
不要只是把這些樣品隨機的發出去。

- **characteristic** (*n.*) [ˌkærəktəˋrɪstɪk] 特徵，特性
What are some **characteristics** of our potential customers?
我們的潛在客戶有些什麼特性呢?

- **respondent** (*n.*) [rɪˋspɑndənt] 受訪者，應答者
Only 10% of **respondents** answered yes to that survey question.
只有百分之十的受訪者對那一題調查的問題答「是」。

- **incline** (*v.*) [ɪnˋklaɪn] 點頭，傾向
From my own experiences, I am **inclined** to disagree.
以我自己的經驗，我傾向不同意。

- **trendy** (*a.*) [ˋtrɛndɪ] 時髦的，流行的
I think they are **trendy** and attractive.
我認為他們很時髦且有吸引力。

有料句型 *Sentence Pattern*

句型 1 ↘

Prior to... 在…之前（應該先…）

Prior to a product or brand launch, a concept test will be conducted.
在一個產品上市之前，針對了目標消費群進行分析。

Prior to breakfast, we should brush the teeth.
在吃早餐之前，我們應該刷牙。

Prior to cooking, she would go shopping first.
在開始煮飯之前，她會先去買菜。

Prior to press conference, make sure all journalists are invited.

在記者會前，要確定已邀約了所有的記者。

句型 2 ↘

... could turn out to be... 很可能演變成⋯

It could very well turn out not to be a single group with a similar background.

它很有可能演變成具有相似背景的單一團體。

It could very well turn out to be true.

這很有可能會變成事實。

It could turn out to be a good thing.

這結果可能是件好事。

句型 3 ↘

A suits B better. A 比較適合 B

That seems to **suit** "Classic & Tradition" **better**.

那似乎比較適合「經典&傳統」（這個主題）。

This dress **suits** her **better**.

這件洋裝比較適合她。

The dance music **suits** the party **better**.

舞曲比較適合這個派對。

Expert Tips
知識補給

The background check and market potential survey are usually conducted at the early stage before the products are released. Based on that, the marketing department is aware of how to communication with the crowd in the near future. Preliminarily, the marketing department develops the concept. Through the concept test, they are informed of the consumers' acceptance. Sometimes the brand endorser's preferences, product design with different shapes, promotions, packages, functions, mouthful tastes, fragrances, distributions and so on.

背景調查與市場潛力調查，通常會發生在品牌上市前最早的階段，讓行銷部知道未來要對什麼樣背景的群眾溝通。初步，行銷部會提出上市行銷主題的概念發想，透過概念測試，得知消費者對於這樣產品上市的溝通，會不會買單。有時候概念測試也會測試代言人喜好度、或不同的設計形狀、促銷組合、包裝、效／功能、口感、香味、銷售方式等等，對消費者進行詢問。

Dialogue 2　延伸對話　　　　　　　　　◎06

Who Should Be The Target Audience of Canned Coffee?
誰才是罐裝咖啡的目標族群？

 情境說明 *Situation*

Katty and Jay are co-workers. They are discussing about who should be the target audience of canned coffee product.

凱蒂與杰是同事。他們正在討論關於誰才是罐裝咖啡的目標族群。

♀♂角色介紹 *Characters*

Katty: Product Marketing Specialist
Jay: Product Marketing Specialist

凱蒂：產品行銷專員
杰：產品行銷專員

 情境對話 *Dialogue*

Katty: Hi, Jay. <u>Do you have a minute?</u>

凱蒂：嗨，杰。有空嗎？

Jay: Wait a second, I have to send this E-Mail now. Okay, shoot. <u>What can I do for you?</u>

杰：等等，我必須現在把這封信發出去。好了，說吧。有什麼我可以幫妳的？

Katty: I think you can help me with this. This market research pointed it out that

凱蒂：我想你可以幫我釐清一下，這份市調說我們的罐

our canned coffee should target office workers as our sales target.

装飲料應該以上班族為主要銷售對象。

Jay: It sounds reasonable.

杰：聽起來很合理。

Katty: Well, I was thinking maybe students also like to drink it.

凱蒂：我原先的想法是學生也會喜歡喝的。

Jay: I don't know about that. According to recent media report, teenagers often consume soft drinks.

杰：我不曉得。因為根據最近的媒體報導，青少年經常喝的飲料是碳酸飲料。

Katty: Well, this sounds also reasonable.

凱蒂：嗯，也有道理。

Jay: If nothing else, I'll see you at lunch.

杰：沒有其他事的話，中午吃飯見囉。

Katty: Yes. See you later.

凱蒂：好。晚點見。

短句補給 Useful Phrases

✓ Do you have a minute? 你有空嗎？
✓ What can I do for you? 我能幫你什麼忙嗎？
✓ I don't know about that. 那個我不知道欸。

品牌策略
Brand Strategy

Brand positioning is like putting clothes on a person. We give them personality, <u>we decide the tone and manner</u>, we tell them what to say, and we create their style and preferences. No wonder sometimes people say that launching a brand is exactly like giving birth to a child.

品牌定位就像是給一個人穿衣服；我們賦予它個性，我們告訴它用什麼口氣說話，我們決定它說什麼話，我們創造它的偏好與品味。難怪有人說，催生一個全新的品牌的上市，就像是自己生了一個孩子一樣辛苦。

1 行銷

2 廣告

3 媒體採購

4 公關公司

5 網路行銷

6 企業社會形象

Dialogue 1　主題對話

Launching a New Brand Is Like Giving Birth to a Child!
為一個品牌催生，就像是生個小孩一樣辛苦！

 情境說明 *Situation*

The Brand Strategy meeting will be in session in a minute. The agency is using the marketing analysis report as a basis to develop a brand and communication strategy suggestion.

品牌策略會議即將開始，廣告公司將依市場分析報告所呈現的結果，提出品牌策略與溝通策略的建議。

情境對話 *Dialogue*

Agency: This is a saturated and stable market in Taiwan, the total vehicle amount shows slow growth since 1998, and the estimation of total amount shows the future negative growth. The marketing analysis indicates that consumers value the following features most highly: Multi-functional, Fuel efficiency, Green Technology, Good Engine Performance, Japanese Fashion Style. Given the situation that we are facing, we need a breakthrough in the oligopoly market. Is there any unmet need among existing car

廣告公司：這其實是一個穩定又飽和的市場。自 1998 年起汽車總數的年成長即呈現很緩慢的趨勢，甚至有預估未來汽車市場將呈現負成長。市場調查的結果顯示，消費者偏好一部多功能性、省油、環保節能、引擎性能佳、日式時尚感設計的車。面對這樣的環境狀況，我們需要有個突破點，來對應這個有點壟斷飽和的市場。是否還有些需求沒有被注意

45

owners that yearns to be satisfied? Or, should we approach a new segment out of the current market? We say, the brand position is "European Premium Masterpiece" and the brand statement is "The European inheritance provides a distinguishing personal image. The premium masterpiece that releases your soul and imagination and unlocks the passion in your life journey."

Manager: What is our target audience (TA) like? What kind of people are they?

Agency: I would say they are The Image Seeker - Age 28~45, with the male to female ratio being skewed 70% to 30%. They are already owners of four-wheelers with more disposable income, having a personal annual income of 1000,000 or above. They take pride and care in their appearance and cosmopolitan self-image. They are at ease while getting together with friends, but they enjoy and cherish even more their own private time and space. They are early adopters who search information and study before they purchase. They exercise careful discern-

到、滿足到？ 又或者，我們應該提供與市場上完全不同的產品訴求？ 我説，這個品牌的定位是「源自歐洲頂級傑作」，品牌宣言則是「承襲經典歐洲車款，獨特原創的個性，這款頂級傑作將釋放出你潛藏在內心自我，陪你開創超乎想像的絕妙旅程」。

經理：我們的潛在消費者是哪種類型？

廣告公司：我們認為會是一群視覺愛好者。年齡在 18 到 45 歲之間，男性為主，男女比例約為七比三，已經擁有汽車，手邊有較多可支配的金錢，年收入在一百萬或以上，穿著有自信且精心打扮，注意個人形象，具國際性的觀點；和朋友聚會會表現得很自在輕鬆，但是也很注重個人隱私與獨處時間，他們注意新事物，購物前通常也會研究一番，有敏銳的洞察力與高雅品味；閱

1 行銷　1-4 品牌策略

1 行銷

2 廣告

3 媒體採購

4 公關公司

5 網路行銷

6 企業社會形象

ment in choosing what to use and wear. They read male fashion magazines and special interest magazines about cars, interior design, watches, cameras, and so on. They are persistent in the detailed refinement of goods and enjoy collecting items such as wine, whisky, watches, bikes and cameras. They are gourmands who enjoy fine cuisine and go to cigar bars and wine houses. They travel overseas and take domestic trips as well. They carry Samsonite / Rimowa luggage. They have a passion for photography and own high-end cameras such as Leica or SONY. They appreciate art and go to art exhibitions and live performances. They mostly shop at department store or shop on the Internet. They play sports, such as biking, golfing and gym visits and they watch sports programs. They are heavy Internet users, spending more than 20 hours a week surfing the internet on computers and mobile devices. Facebook is the one of most common internet platforms for sharing / exchanging information and ideas.

Manager: I think we need to discuss this

讀男性時尚雜誌，也特別對車、設計、手錶、攝影類的雜誌很有興趣，堅持做工精細的精良物件，也會熱衷收集酒類、手錶、腳踏車與照相機，是個美食家會去雪茄屋及品酒。他們會在國內外四處旅行。他們用的是新秀麗或是日默瓦行李箱。對於攝影有很高的熱情，擁有設備精良的攝影機如徠卡或SONY，對於藝術品特別賞識與領會，會參觀藝術展覽與現場表演，大多在百貨公司內消費，或是在網路上消費，喜歡看或參與運動活動－腳踏車、高爾夫或健身房，是重度網路使用者，每週用電腦或手機上網超過20 小時以上，臉書更是其中一個最常被使用的網路分享或交換訊息與創意的平台。

經理：我想我們需要內部討

issue internally and decide the appropriate brand statement and position. As for the brand strategy, I would suggest "provide the most premium products to make youngest desire to own and increase the market share 2% in 2015." Moreover, the communication strategy will be delivered when we agreed the TA persona as you described.

論一下，再來確認品牌宣言與定位。至於品牌策略，我建議「提供一個最精良的產品讓年輕族群期待渴望擁有；並可以在 2015 年達到市占率成長 2%」，此外，溝通策略的方向，依剛剛所提出的潛在消費者的輪廓，待我們同意後再提出。

ABC 有料字彙 Vocabulary

- **saturate** (v.) [ˋsætʃəˌret] 飽和，充滿
  The current market is **saturated** and slowing.
  目前市場呈現飽和及成長趨緩的狀態。

- **breakthrough** (n.) [ˋbrekˌθru] 突破性進展，突破點
  They have made a **breakthrough** in developing this product.
  他們在發展這項產品上已有重大突破。

- **oligopoly** (n.) [ˌɑləˋgɑpəlɪ] 供過於求
  The mobile phone market has a trend toward **oligopoly**.
  手機市場有供過於求的趨勢。

- **unmet** (a.) [ʌnˋmɛt] 未被滿足的
  We will do our best to satisfy those **unmet** needs.
  我們會盡全力滿足那些未被滿足的需求。

- **inheritance** (*n.*) [ɪn`hɛrɪtəns] 承襲，傳統
  He received a large **inheritance**.
  他得到一大筆遺產。

- **masterpiece** (*n.*) [`mæstɚˌpis] 傑作，名品
  His brilliant marketing strategy turns this junk into a **masterpiece**.
  他絕妙的行銷策略把這破爛變成傑作。

- **skewed** (*a.*) [skjud] 被曲解為，被區分為
  The news report is being **skewed** toward one political viewpoint.
  這新聞報導被曲解為單一政治觀點。

- **disposable** (*a.*) [dɪ`spozəb!] 可任意支配使用的
  Our potential customers will be those who have enough **disposable** income to buy the product.
  我們的潛在客戶會是那些有足夠收入購買產品並可任意支配使用的人。

- **cosmopolitan** (*a.*) [ˌkazmə`palətn] 世界性的，國際性的
  Taipei is a **cosmopolitan** city.
  台北市是一個國際性的城市。

- **discernment** (*n.*) [dɪ`sɝnmənt] 洞察力，識別力
  She showed great **discernment** in her choice of men.
  她對選男人的洞察力很高。

- **persistent** (*a.*) [pɚ`sɪstənt] 堅持的，固執的
  Some consumers report **persistent** problems when they try to log in.
  有些消費者回報說登入時有持續的問題。

- **refinement** (*n.*) [rɪ`faɪnmənt] 高雅，精緻
  The new product has **refinements** that worth your attention.
  這新產品有精緻的設備，值得關注。

- **gourmand** (*n.*) [ˋɡʊrmənd] 老饕，美食家
  The restaurant attracts **gourmands** from around the world.
  這餐廳吸引來自世界各地的美食家。

 **有料句型** *Sentence Pattern*

句型 1 ↘

the tone and manner

一般被翻譯為語氣與態度，但是也可以時常拿來形容氣氛與方式

We decide **the tone and manner**.
我們決定氣氛與方式。

What is **the tone and manner** of the event?
這個活動的氣氛是如何？

What is **the tone and manner** of the brand?
這個品牌的調性是如何？

句型 2 ↘

A exercise careful discernment in B.　A 在 B 方面仔細嚴格地⋯。

They **exercise careful discernment in** choosing what to use and wear.
他們在所使用的物品及穿著打扮上會仔細嚴格地選擇。

How can we **exercise discernment in** people around us?
我們該如何慎選在我們身邊的朋友？

He **exercises careful discernment in** choosing what to eat.
他對挑選吃什麼食物有很高的鑑賞力。

Expert Tips
知識補給

When outlining brand strategies and profiling consumers, we usually compare one or two brands with different product homogeneity. For example, we could say that those who own imported cars are also those who use Leica cameras. Leica cameras is a high-end, legacy brand to get to know our own brand rankings among the homogeneity products and future directions. Besides, after the potential consumers are profiled, the communication arrangement and media buying for specific magazines and internet are about to get started.

在寫品牌策略或是形容潛在消費者的輪廓時，經常會比擬一兩個知名的非同質性產品的品牌，如我們的進口車主即為徠卡相機使用者，徠卡相機在相機市場是高價位、且是有傳承歷史的品牌，此時，便可以更清楚了解我們自己品牌在同質性產品中的位階、未來要走的路線。另外，當潛在消費者的輪廓確認後，便可以針對這些人平時可能會接觸到媒體，如特定的雜誌與網路等，安排溝通計劃與媒體購買。

Dialogue 2　延伸對話 08

What Does a Brand Strategy Cover? 品牌策略包含哪些?

 情境說明 *Situation*

Peter and Sean are sitting at Peter's office, and discussing the brand strategy of the new product.

彼特和西恩正在彼特的辦公室討論公司一款新產品的品牌策略。

♀♂**角色介紹** *Characters*

Peter: Brand Manager
Sean: Brand Management Specialist

彼特：品牌經理
西恩：品牌管理專員

💬 **情境對話** *Dialogue*

Peter: Sean, have we got the survey report which we asked the marketing research firm to do?

Sean: Yes, Boss. This marketing analysis shows that most candidates agreed that we named our new product "ABC."

Peter: Really? Clear and easy to remember, isn't it?

Sean: Indeed. Moreover, <u>there are more than half</u> candidates said that they prefer

彼特：西恩，我們請市調公司做的調查報告出爐了嗎？

西恩：有的，主管。根據這份報告，大多數受訪者贊成新產品取名叫 ABC。

彼特：是嗎？清楚又好記，不是嗎？

西恩：是的。還有，有超過半數的受訪者表示他們喜歡

Logo A.

A 款的品牌 LOGO。

Peter: It looks like that female consumers prefer bright colored and streamline shape design.

彼特：看來女性消費者還是比較偏好顏色明亮，流線造型的設計。

Sean: It sounds like this. Besides that, there are more than seventy percent of candidates agreed with organic appeal of the new product.

西恩：看起來是這樣沒錯。另外，超過7成的受訪者，對於新產品的有機訴求表示認同。

Peter: Great! Is there anything else?

彼特：太棒了！還有其他的嗎？

Sean: Yes. It is unbelievable that there are ninety percent of candidates suggested us to design a cartoon character, as our brand spokesman to create a friendly image.

西恩：有的。你一定想不到有九成的受訪者建議我們設計一個卡通造型，成為品牌代言人，便於營造友善的感覺。

Peter: Seriously? It's really beyond my expectation.

彼特：認真的嗎？這個可出乎我的意料之外呢。

短句補給 Useful Phrases

✓ There are more than half... 有超過半數的…
✓ Is there anything else? 還有其他的嗎？
✓ It's really beyond my expectation. 這真出乎我的意料之外。

1-5 品牌策略調整
Brand Strategy Adjustment

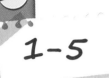

Recently, the media covered some negative news about our brand. The sales numbers have been dropping since the news outbreak. We are all very worried as the issue of brand trust has been a persistent problem that did not begin just yesterday.

　　近來，媒體報導了許多關於我們品牌的負面新聞，而銷售數字也自該新聞爆發以來，持續下滑。對於外界對我們品牌的信任度，大家都非常擔心，但是這個問題的存在已經不是一兩天的事了。

Dialogue 1　主題對話

The Problem Did Not Begin Just Yesterday!
這問題已經不是一天兩天的事了！

 情境說明 *Situation*

All department directors are gathering for the meeting named "Regain Brand Trust." The host will be the marketing director and she is about to start the meeting.

所有部門的主管正聚在一起，共同參加一場名為「重建品牌信任」的會議，會議將由行銷部的總監主持，而現在會議正要開始。

情境對話 *Dialogue*

Marketing Director: As we are all aware, the negative news impacts our sales tremendously. We really need to look into the issue and revisit the brand strategy to evaluate if there is a need to adjust it. Every participant please share your observations and comments concerning the brand strategy as it relates to brand trust.

行銷總監：大家近來都注意到，那些負面新聞的報導正嚴重影響著我們的營收業績。我們真的需要正視這個問題點，以及重新檢視品牌策略，評估是否有調整策略的急迫性。每一位與會者都請分享你們對於品牌信任之於品牌策略的觀察與意見。

Sales Director: Our brand strategy is "delivery of consistent good taste and well designed food throughout the world to

業務總監：我們的品牌策略為『在全球每一個角落都提供一致美味與擺盤裝飾的食

become the top of mind family restaurant with incremental sales of 2 billion by 2020." I think parents usually play the role of gatekeepers for food safety and quality. Without their trust of our brand, perhaps we can still achieve the sales target from youngsters, but it will be very hard to become a family loved restaurant.

PR Director: Indeed. I think we should stop passively responding to the negative news, and on the contrary, I suggest we communicate aggressively to the public about our high standard of food safety. This could be the first step of building up the brand trust.

Marketing Director: Agree. Back to brand strategy, since we all think that brand trust is a serious issue that we need to overcome from all perspectives, I suggest that we adjust the brand strategy as "delivery of consistent good taste, well designed and people trusted product throughout the world to become the top of mind family restaurant with incremental sales of 2 billion by 2020."

品，並成為首屈一指的家庭最愛餐廳，於 2020 年時可增加二十億的營業額。』，然而我認為，家長通常扮演對食品安全與品質把關的角色，如果無法得到他們對我們品牌的信任，也許我們仍然透過年輕族群的消費，達到目標營業額，但我們將很難成為一個家庭最愛餐廳。

公關總監：的確，關於那些負面新聞，我想我們必須停止被動式的對應。相反地，我建議我們應該積極主動的向大眾溝通，我們對品管要求的高標準。這可以成為重建品牌信任的第一步。

行銷總監：同意。再講回品牌策略的部分，既然我們都同意品牌信任度是一個重要的議題，且必須從每一個觀點來關注，我建議要將品牌策略調整為『在全球每一個角落都提供一致美味、擺盤裝飾與人們信任的食品，並成為首屈一指的家庭最愛餐廳，於 2020 年時可增加二十億的營業額。』

1 行銷

2 廣告

3 媒體採購

4 公關公司

5 網路行銷

6 企業社會形象

Sales Director: So I will call a national sales meeting to express our new goal and objective to build the brand trust. We will actively explain to consumers our high food standards, the principle of "cook after ordering," our method of maintaining a hygienic and clean environment, and so on.

業務總監：如此一來，我會召開全國業務大會來說明我們新目標與主旨 – 建立品牌信任。主動向消費者解釋，我們食物的品質標準；而且，我們都是收到點餐訂單後，才開始料理；我們如何維持環境衛生整潔等等。

PR Director: I will pitch some quality TV talking shows for introducing our ingredients sourcing and how the farmers grow it.

公關總監：我會向電視台一些談話性節目邀約訪問，介紹一下關於我們原物料來源，以及農夫們是如何種植它們的。

Marketing Director: I will create two TVCs about our global quality standards and how we educate and train restaurant staff to follow the standards. I will also design a small stand board next to our counters to promote the awareness.

行銷總監：我會製作兩支電視廣告，讓大家認識我們全球品管標準，與我們是如何訓練員工務必遵守這些標準。此外，還會製作一小立牌放在結賬櫃檯旁，達到增加認知的目的。

HR Director: I will then conduct a series of training sessions for all our staff, in order to enhance the understanding of how we value the food quality and our safety standards.

人事總監：我這裡便會舉辦幾場教育訓練，向全員工重申我們有多重視食物安全與品質的標準。

Managing Director: <u>We came out with a very promising</u> solution today. I will report to Asia Pacific regional head about our strategy adjustment and follow-up approaches later.

總經理：我們今天提出了一個很有力度的解決之道。稍晚，我會向亞太區的主管報告，關於我們品牌策略的調整與接下來的配合步驟。

ABC 有料字彙 *Vocabulary*

- **tremendously** (*adv.*) [trɪˋmɛndəslɪ] 極度地，非常地
  This database is **tremendously** large.
  這資料庫非常地龐大。

- **incremental** (*a.*) [ˏɪnkrəˋmənt!] 增值的，增加的
  That purse may be costly in comparison to her total income, but it will be **incremental**.
  跟她的總收入比較起來那包包或許很昂貴，但它是會增值的。

- **gatekeeper** (*n.*) [ˋgetˏkipɚ] 守門人，把關者
  Please be the **gatekeepers** of your personal information.
  請做個人資料的守門員（為個人資料把關）。

- **youngsters** (*n.*) [ˋjʌŋstɚ] 年輕人，小孩
  One day, you may share your experience with these **youngsters**.
  有一天，你可以和這些年輕人一起分享經驗。

- **passively** (*adv.*) [ˋpæsɪvlɪ] 被動地，順從地
  You may defend yourself actively, or accept it **passively**.
  你可以主動為自己辯護，或被動接受一切。

- **contrary** (*n.*) [ˋkɑntrɛrɪ] 相反，對立
  It's not user-friendly at all. On the **contrary**, I found it very

difficult to operate.

它一點都沒有「使用者友善」設計。相反地，我發現它很難操作。

- **overcome** (*v.*) [ˌovəˋkʌm] 克服，戰勝
The R&D Team has many obstacles to **overcome**.
研發小組有許多障礙需要克服。

- **throughout** (*prep.*) [θruˋaʊt] 遍佈，貫穿
The fragrance persisted **throughout** the day.
這香味持續了一整天。

- **hygienic** (*a.*) [ˌhaɪdʒɪˋɛnɪk] 衛生的
People always want the food they are eating to be **hygienic** and safe.
人都想要吃進去的食物是衛生安全的。

- **promising** (*a.*) [ˋprɑmɪsɪŋ] 有希望的，大有可為的
He looks so young and **promising** that many job opportunities and pretty girls await him.
他看起來是如此地年輕有前途，許多工作機會和漂亮女孩都在等著他。

有料句型 Sentence Pattern

句型 1 ↘

top of mind　心目中排名第一的

It becomes **the top of mind** family restaurant.
它變成了大家心目中排名第一的家庭餐廳。

My **top of mind** country to go is Japan.
我心目中最想去的國家是日本。

This is the most **top of mind** brand for public.
這是個大眾心目中第一的品牌。

句型 2 ↘

A come out with a adj. B. 從 A 出來一個 B。

We **came out with a** very promising solution today.
我們今天想出一個很棒的解決之道。

He **came out with a** creative design.
他做出一個很有創意的設計。

I **came out with** some special ideas.
我想出一些很特別的點子。

Expert Tips
知識補給

A brand strategy is a long term plan, usually short and to the point. It usually goes through a time period of three or five years. Once being confirmed, it is not supposed to have big variations or drastically changes in three to five years. Usually, a repositioning is needed when it comes to the following situations: poor sales volume, negative coverage, and low popularity. At this moment, it means that the following aspects are also needed to be checked: brand maturity, consumer trust, brand identification, and brand name (whether it's easy to recognize and memorize or not). Meanwhile, public relations, pricing, and distribution strategies are being reviewed as well.

品牌策略是一個長遠的規劃，通常只會是一個簡短的概要，策略都會以三年或五年來看，通常一旦經過確認，三至五年內應該不會有大幅度的變化或更動。而一個品牌的策略會需要被重新定位，通常主要發生在下面三種情況時：品牌銷售不佳、品牌負面新聞過多、品牌知名度低。這時，通常需要被檢視的地方則是：品牌年輕度或成熟度、受消費者信任度、品牌認同、品牌名稱（容易辨識與記憶與否等），而公關、定價與通路策略亦會被同時檢視。

61

Dialogue 2　延伸對話　10

Make a Combination of Spirit And Dreams.
結合品牌精神與夢想

☕ 情境說明 *Situation*

Katherine is a Brand Manager, and Andy is an Advertising Manager. They are talking about the brand strategy contents which are going to be adjusted.

凱薩琳是品牌經理，安迪是廣告經理。他們正在討論即將對品牌策略調整的內容。

♀♂ 角色介紹 *Characters*

Katherine: Brand Manager
Andy: Advertising Manager

凱薩琳：品牌經理
安迪：廣告經理

情境對話 *Dialogue*

Katherine: Andy! <u>Congratulations on your promotion!</u>
Andy: Thanks a lot. By the way, I heard that we are going to set up a new brand strategy?
Katherine: Indeed. I am going to redefine our brand and give it a new image.

凱薩琳：安迪！恭喜你升遷了！
安迪：十分感謝。對了，聽說最近公司有制定新的品牌策略？
凱薩琳：的確。我打算將品牌重新詮釋，賦予新的形象。

1 行銷　1-5 品牌策略調整

1 行銷

2 廣告

3 媒體採購

4 公關公司

5 網路行銷

6 企業社會形象

Andy: Such as?

Katherine: There are many people talking about <u>dream dreams and ready to pay the price to make them come true.</u> So I am going to make a combination of our brand sprit and "dreams."

Andy: Well, this is a good idea. <u>Dreams are always make people blood boil</u>, and give people a feeling of "<u>get up and go!</u>"

Katherine: That's right. And this is exactly matches the feature of our products.

Andy: You know I am always there for you, so if there is anything you need me, just give me a call.

Katherine: You bet!

安迪：舉例來說呢？

凱薩琳：最近很多人在談論勇敢追夢。所以我打算將品牌的精神與「夢想」做結合。

安迪：嗯，這是個好點子。夢想總是讓人感到熱血沸騰，而且給人「積極去做吧！」的一種感覺。

凱薩琳：是的。正符合我們的產品的特性。

安迪：妳知道我隨時支援妳，所以有需要我的地方，儘管打電話給我。

凱薩琳：沒問題！

短句補給 *Useful Phrases*

✓ Congratulations on your promotion! 恭喜你升遷！

✓ Dream dreams and ready to pay the price to make them come true. 勇敢追夢。

✓ Dreams are always make people blood boil. 夢想總是讓人感到熱血沸騰。

✓ Get up and go. 積極去執行。

產品價格與促銷
Price & Promotion

Projection setting is the hardest part when planning a promotion. This is true even when the projection is made by experienced marketers; it does not always meet the real sales number.

當計劃一個促銷活動是，設定預計銷售數字是最難的部分。我知道就算是由經驗豐富的行銷人設定出的預計銷售數字，仍有可能不會總是符合實際銷售的數字。

1 行銷

2 廣告

3 媒體採購

4 公關公司

5 網路行銷

6 企業社會形象

Dialogue 1　主題對話

This Is The Hardest Part! 這是最困難的部分了！

情境說明 _Situation_

It's about time to set up the price and confirm all the promotion mechanisms. A promotion plan is drafted and discussed in a meeting with other department heads. The marketing specialist is now making the first draft of the plan.

是時候該定出產品價格與確認所有促銷的活動方法，行銷部該提出一個促銷活動計劃，然後再與其他部門主管開會討論，此時行銷專員正在擬定計劃的大致內容。

情境對話 _Dialogue_

Tom: Before preparing the promotion plan, I would like to have a discussion with you in order to reach some kind of initial consensus.

湯姆：在開始準備計劃之前，我想先與您有個討論，以便達到初步共識。

Marketing Manager: Yes, did you get the prime cost from the finance department for each product?

行銷經理：好的，你有從會記部門先取得產品個別的成本了嗎？

Tom: I did. This promotion campaign includes three products-- jelly soda, seafood salad, and chicken rice. The prime costs for them are $5, $16 and $23 respectively.

湯姆：我拿到了。這次的活動包含了三樣產品促銷，果凍蘇打、海鮮沙拉與香雞飯。三樣產品的成本為五元、十六元及二十三元。

Marketing Manager: The gross profit margin hopefully will stay around 55%.

Tom: I know, so I am setting the price as $30, $85 and $110 respectively.

Marketing Manager: Don't you think the price for chicken rice is too low? It's less than 50%.

Tom: Yes, it's lower than 50%. But we need to offer something to make the consumer feel that coming here to dine is a good value for the money. You could see the chicken rice as a guest count driver.

Marketing manager: Regarding the promotion period, should we go for three weeks or four weeks?

Tom: I would say three weeks. Based on past experience, the sales come in very slow from week three. Besides, we don't have the budget to do TVC until the 4th week.

Marketing Manager: Agree. Shall we start the promotion from June 1st?

Tom: I would like to start the promotion from June 2nd to 22nd, since June 2nd is the Dragon Boat Festival. More consumers

行銷經理：希望毛利率可以維持在大約百分之五十五。

湯姆：我知道，所以我將產品定價為三十元、八十五元及一百一十元。

行銷經理：你不覺得香雞飯的價格有點低嗎？ 低於百分之五十。

湯姆：是的，確實低於百分之五十。但是我們需要讓消費者感覺，來我們這邊用餐物超所值，有些產品就是這樣的目的，你可以把香雞飯當成刺激來客增加的商品。

行銷經理：關於促銷活動的期間，我們應該執行三週或是四週呢？

湯姆：我會建議三週，因為根據過去的經驗，通常第三週期，銷售數字就會降低很多，此外，我們並沒有足夠的預算，讓電視廣告延續到第四週。

行銷經理：同意，那我們是否在六月一日開始活動？

湯姆：我想要在六月二日開始，活動期間到六月二十二日，因為六月二日是端午

1 行銷

2 廣告

3 媒體採購

4 公關公司

5 網路行銷

6 企業社會形象

would come to stores that day. And the last day is the 22nd, which is a Sunday, and the stores would have better crowds on that day as well.

Marketing Manager: Great idea. As for the mechanism, I really think it should be easier.

Tom: Yes, maybe the mechanism can be "upload the receipt of any new promotion product to the event website, you will get one free premium."

Marketing Manager: What is the premium?

Tom: It would be a green tea cake coupon, since that cake is a slow-moving product.

Marketing Manager: What is your selling projection for the three products, and how many cake coupons would you print?

Tom: My target is 20,000 for jelly soda, 6500 for seafood salad and 2,800 for chicken rice in three weeks. I base this on the fact that a soda can be purchased with all meals, and according to the weekly

節，當天會有很多來店客，而活動的最後一天是二十二日，也剛好是個星期天，店內會有較多的人潮來衝最後一天的業績。

行銷經理：很好的意見。至於活動的規則，我真的認為應該要更簡單一點。

湯姆：活動規則會是「上傳購買任一新產品的發票到活動網站，即可得到免費的贈品一份」。

行銷經理：活動贈品是什麼？

湯姆：將會是綠茶蛋糕兌換券，因為綠茶蛋糕是我們滯銷的產品。

行銷經理：關於這三個新產品，你的預期銷售數字是如何？ 還有你打算印多少張蛋糕兌換券？

湯姆：我的目標是 20,000 杯果凍蘇打，6,500 個海鮮沙拉，2,800 份香雞飯。因為所有的餐點都可以點一杯蘇打，根據每週的銷售數字

sales report, the average number of sales of other flavor soda per week is about 7,000 cups. And the number for salad, I base this on the sales record from Hong Kong where they launched it last month. As for the chicken rice, we had a similar chicken product last year but with a different flavor. So I adopted the actual sales numbers of our chicken product last year to do the projection. Therefore, I suggest that we print 20,000 coupons since the redemption rate is usually around 55%.

Marketing Manager: Please do include the prime cost of 20,000 cakes into our promotion campaign spending.

來看，別的口味的蘇打每週平均銷售 7,000 杯；至於沙拉的數字，我是根據上個月香港上市時的數字來推估；而香雞飯，我們曾經在去年上市過類似的雞肉產品，只是當時口味不太一樣，所以我採用了去年實際的雞肉商品銷售量，來設定預定銷售數字。因此，我建議印製 20,000 張兌換券，因為一般來說的兌換率為百分之五十五。

行銷經理：請將二萬份的蛋糕成本，也加到我們整個活動的花費裡。

ABC 有料字彙 Vocabulary

- **consensus** (*n.*) [kənˋsɛnsəs] 一致共識
  Finally we reached a **consensus** at the meeting this morning.
  終於我們在今早的會議中達成共識。

- **respectively** (*adv.*) [rɪˋspɛktɪvlɪ] 分別地，各自地
  These two online commercials attracted 6 thousand and 2 million viewers, **respectively**.
  這兩支線上廣告分別吸引了六千及兩百萬人觀賞。

- **mechanism** (*n.*) [ˈmɛkəˌnɪzəm] 機制，辦法
  The company needs better **mechanisms** to response to radical innovation.
  這公司需要更佳的機制以回應劇烈的創新。

- **crowd** (*n.*) [kraʊd] 人群
  The brand you build has to stand out from the **crowd**.
  妳所建立的品牌必須從人群中脫穎而出。

- **premium** (*n.*) [ˈprimɪəm] 獎品，獎金
  You may take the phone home as a **premium** after the show.
  表演結束後，你可以把這支電話當作獎品帶回家。

- **slow-moving** 滯銷的，流動慢的
  An outstanding marketing team is what you need during this **slow-moving** economic recovery.
  在這緩慢的經濟復甦期間，你需要的是一個傑出的行銷團隊。

- **redemption** (*n.*) [rɪˈdɛmpʃən] 兌換，贖回
  Some brands with bad reputations are ready for a little **redemption**.
  一些聲譽不佳的品牌已經準備好來點小小的救贖。

有料句型 Sentence Pattern

句型 1 ↘

A base B on the fact that...　A 基於 B 的事實（去…）

We **base this on the fact that** a soda can be purchased with all meals.
我們是基於「汽水能搭配任何餐點做銷售的事實」去做成結論的。

Decisions are **based on the fact that** the brain retrieves existing information from the past.
做決定，是大腦根據過去存在的資訊的判斷。

I will **base on** the sales number yesterday to order the stock for tomorrow.
我會根據昨天的銷售數字，去訂明天的存貨。

句型 2 ↘

A meet B　A 達到 B（標準／期望／預估...）

The projection does not always **meet** the real sales number.
預估並不總是等於實際銷售數字。

The sales numbers should **meet** the projection.
銷售數字應該要符合預估。

I don't know how to **meet** the company expectation.
我不知道如何達成公司期望。

Expert Tips
知識補給

Each brand has different gross profit margin. There's no standard. Besides, it's not an easy job to set the sales numbers to meet the real ones. Those numbers are being not only supported by concrete references, but also persuasive enough to convince superiors from different departments. When it comes to free gifts, the quality should be paid more attention to if they are outsourcing products in order to avoid unnecessary disputes with consumers.

每一個品牌與公司的毛利率標準設定是不一樣的，沒有一定的標準；此外，設定預期銷售目標數字更不是件容易的工作，這些數字不但要有明確的參考依據，更要能夠足以說服公司各部門的主管；贈品如果不是自家公司的產品，通常要注意品質，避免事後消費者對該贈品品質有疑慮時，發生不必要的糾紛。

Dialogue 2　延伸對話　　　　　　　🔘 12

What Kinds of Products Need to Be Promoted All the Time?
什麼產品需要經常促銷？

 情境說明 *Situation*

Helen and Kevin are arguing the price and promotion event of toilet paper.

海倫與凱文正在爭論衛生紙的價格與促銷活動。

♀♂ **角色介紹** *Characters*

Helen: Promotion Specialist
Kevin: Product Specialist

海倫：促銷活動專員
凱文：產品專員

💬 **情境對話** *Dialogue*

Helen: I just don't understand why we have to plan one promotion after another for selling toilet paper.

海倫：我實在不了解為什麼衛生紙要一直規劃促銷活動。

Kevin: This is because we have to <u>increase the sales volume</u>.

凱文：這是因為要盡量增加銷售量。

Helen: I think our company has good sales volume already.

海倫：我想我們公司的銷售量已經很好了吧。

Kevin: Consumers could continue to remember our brand through regular promotion events.

凱文：經常辦促銷活動，也可以讓消費者持續記得我們品牌啊。

Helen: But some luxury jewelry brands are not doing this often.

海倫：但是高價的珠寶商品就很少辦促銷活動。

Kevin: Luxurious goods tend to be low price elastic. Jewelry buyers <u>care more about</u> the value increments or brand image than its buying price.

凱文：這是因為珠寶是價格彈性小的商品。買珠寶的人對買進價格不見得很在乎，反而是考慮增值或者品牌形象等。

Helen: <u>It makes sense.</u>

海倫：聽起來有點道理。

Kevin: Consumer products, such as salt, soy sauce, and toilet paper, on the contrary, are products with high price elasticity of demand. It's easier to attract more consumers through lowering the price, or getting an extra gift in the same price.

凱文：然而低價的民生消費用品，像是鹽、醬油、衛生紙等商品。如果以降價或者同價格但是多了贈品的方式促銷，就容易吸引消費者選購。

短句補給 Useful Phrases

✓ increase the sales volume　增加銷售量
✓ care more about…　對…更關心
✓ It makes sense.　有道理。

1-7

產品測試
Product Testing

When conducting a focus group, the marketing team has to carry out a series of discussions with the research team on a number of issues, including: anticipated concern, marketing potential approaches, and product concept. The hope and goal is to enable the team to develop an appropriate questionnaire of the focus group.

舉辦一場焦點小組訪問，行銷團隊與市調團隊需要經過好幾次的討論，內容包括可預期的顧慮、行銷可能使用的溝通角度與產品概念。希望如此可以讓市調團隊設計出適合的訪問問題。

1 行銷

2 廣告

3 媒體採購

4 公關公司

5 網路行銷

6 企業社會形象

Dialogue 1　主題對話

Which Would Attract You More? 哪個比較吸引你?

 情境說明 *Situation*

The marketing team is now at the research house, and later will be observing the consumer feedback through a dark glass window from a separate room. The topic of focus group today is about new product testing and the theme of communication.

行銷部團隊來到了市調公司的辦公室，稍後將透過另一個房間內的暗色玻璃，觀察消費者的意見與回饋。今天的訪談測試的主題是新口味產品試吃，以及該行銷產品的溝通角度。

情境對話 *Dialogue*

Host: Could you introduce your age and occupation to all participants please?

主持人：能否請你向大家介紹一下自己的年齡與職業？

Male participant: I am a university student, 23 years old.

男性參與者：我是一個大學生，二十三歲。

Female participant: I am a working mom, 34 years old.

女性參與者：我是一個有孩子的職業婦女，三十四歲。

Host: Thank you for coming. Today, we are going to try a new flavor of chocolate. The product name that we are about to try is

主持人：謝謝您們的參與。今天，我們將是吃一個新口味的巧克力，這個產品是由

"Dry Sherry Cherry Chocolate" from XXX brand. The communication approach for this product is "dreaming wild, dreaming sweet." Or "Fruity spring, cherry blooming season" please share with me your preference of product and approaches and explain why.

Male Consumer: I just tried the product and like the level of sweetness. A little bit bitter taste left on my tongue and it has rich sherry aroma. Really enjoy it!

Female Consumer: I think the sherry smell in chocolate is too strong. Maybe only an adult could accept the flavor. The size design is also a bit too big. It's not a mouthful size.

Host: What do you think about the texture?

Male Consumer: I like the fudge-like texture, plus it's neither sticky nor hard to chew.

Female Consumer: I like it too; I always like chewy foods such as bubble tea.

XXX 品牌推出的，名稱叫『櫻桃雪利巧克力』。而行銷溝通的角度有兩個，一個是「夢入狂野，夢飄香甜」，另一個則是「果香春風，櫻花祭」，請告訴我對於產品及這兩個角度的的看法和原因。

男性參與者：我剛剛試吃了產品，很喜歡這樣的甜度。一點點地微苦留在舌尖上，混著雪利酒濃郁的香氣。真的很合我的口味！

女性參與者：我覺得巧克力裡的雪利酒香味太濃了一點。而且，不是一口一個的大小。

主持人：請問你們覺得口感如何？

男性參與者：我喜歡那種類似軟糖般的口感，而且一點也不黏牙，也不會太硬咬不動。

女性參與者：我也喜歡，有嚼勁的食物如珍珠奶茶一直都是我的最愛。

1 行銷

2 廣告

3 媒體採購

4 公關公司

5 網路行銷

6 企業社會形象

Host: Do you smell the sherry from the package?

Female Consumer: Yes, I can smell it before opening it up.

Male Consumer: Not really. I don't smell any sherry but I do smell some fruity cherry.

主持人：你們可以從包裝外聞到雪利的酒香嗎？

女性參與者：可以。我不用拆開包裝就聞得到。

男性參與者：不會耶! 我沒有聞到雪利酒香，但是我聞到一些櫻桃類的水果味。

Host: What do you think about the two different package designs and colors? Do they suit the chocolate?

主持人：對於兩種不同的包裝設計與色調，你們覺得如何？ 與巧克力相配嗎？

Male Consumer: Package design A is very adult driven, mature and clean cut. I like it.

男性參與者：我喜歡 A 款的包裝設計，偏向成人的感覺，成熟且鮮明俐落。

Female Consumer: My kids love chocolate a lot. I think package design B would attract them more, because of the amusing contrast of cold and warm colors.

女性參與者：我的孩子們也很喜歡巧克力，我想 B 款的包裝設計會比較吸引他們，特別是因為暖色和冷色系的有趣對比。

Host: What do you think about the communication themes? Which theme would attract you more: the printing materials and advertisement using "Dreaming wild, Dreaming sweet" or "Fruity Spring, Cherry Blooming Season?"

主持人：請問你們覺得兩個行銷溝通的角度如何？ 哪一個會比較吸引你，當你見到相關印刷傳單與廣告是「夢入狂野，夢飄香甜」，或是「果香春風，櫻花祭」？

Male Consumer: I like the Dreaming

男性參與者：我喜歡夢的那

theme. It's more creative and vibrant to youngsters.

一款，比較生動有創意，會引起年輕人的興趣。

Female Consumer: I like the Fruity Spring.

女性參與者：我喜歡果香春風的角度。

Host: Could you please wait for five minutes and I will be right back.
Host leaves the interview room, and enters the marketing observation room next door.
主持人離開訪談房間，進入位於隔壁的行銷團隊觀察用的房間內。

主持人：能否請你們等我五分鐘，我稍後就回來。

Host: Are there any more questions that I need to follow up on? Otherwise, I will go back and sum up the interview.

主持人：請問還有沒有什麼問題需要我在追問？ 如果沒有，我將回去完結今天的訪談。

Marketing Manager: Yes, before your closure, could you please ask them about the frequency of purchasing chocolate on a regular basis?

行銷經理：有的，在你完結之前，請你能否問一下他們平時購買巧克力的頻率？

Host: No problem.

主持人：沒問題!

ABC 有料字彙 *Vocabulary*

- **anticipate** (*v.*) [æn`tɪsəˌpet] 期望，預料

  It is **anticipated** that the need for cars will grow in the coming years.

  人們預期汽車的需求量近幾年會增加。

- **questionnaire** (*n.*) [ˌkwɛstʃənˋɛr] 問卷，意見調查表
  Open-ended questions, which cannot be answered with a simple "yes" or "no," will come at the end of the **questionnaire**.
  開放式的問題，也就是不能只簡單回答是或否的問題，將會出現在問卷的最後部份。

- **participant** (*n.*) [parˋtɪsəpənt] 參加者，參與者
  For this case, most **participants** who gave negative comments were male.
  就這個案子來說，大部份給予負面評價的參與者是男性。

- **mouthful** (*n.*) [ˋmaʊθfəl] 一口少量
  We will provide a **mouthful** of bread as a sample for each one in the store.
  我們會提供店內每人一口份量的麵包試吃。

- **texture** (*n.*) [ˋtɛkstʃɚ] 口感，質地
  The smooth **texture** is very popular.
  這滑順口感非常受歡迎。

- **chewy** (*a.*) [ˋtʃuɪ] 柔軟有咬勁
  It tastes good, a bit **chewy** though.
  嚐起來味道不錯，雖然要稍微嚼一下。

- **amusing** (*a.*) [əˋmjuzɪŋ] 有趣的，好玩的
  I found it **amusing** when I heard the news.
  當我聽到這新聞時，我感到很有趣。

🐤🐤 有料句型 Sentence Pattern

句型 1 ↘

neither... nor... 既不...也不...

It's **neither** sticky **nor** hard to chew.
它嚼起來既不黏也不硬。

She is **neither** ugly **nor** fat.
她既不醜也不胖。

My notebook is **neither** brand new **nor** very old.
我的電腦不是最新款，但也不是很舊。

句型 2 ↘

on a regular / daily / weekly / monthly / quarterly / yearly basis
定期地（在一個固定週期）/每天/每週/每月/每季/每年

How about the frequency of purchasing chocolate **on a regular basis**?
他們定期購買巧克力的頻率為何？

Please provide a report to me **on a weekly basis**.
請每週提供一份報告給我。

I need a report **on a quarterly basis**.
我需要每季都有一份報告。

They will send the newsletter to all **on a regular basis**.
他們會定期寄出刊物給大家。

1 行銷

2 廣告

3 媒體採購

4 公關公司

5 網路行銷

6 企業社會形象

Expert Tips
知識補給

Consumer testing is also known as "focus group" as well as "concept test." When a consumer testing is conducted, sometimes the brand logo is hidden. For examples, just give the group members three to four kinds of products without telling them which is what brand and ask their preferences respectively. However, sometimes they will try on those products with open data like brand names.

同樣的消費者測試,有的公司稱之為 Focus Group(焦點小組訪問),有的公司稱為 Concept Test(消費者測試),有些時候不會對消費者透露出品牌,比如說同類型產品的三至四種品牌,一一詢問消費者對個別的喜好;但有時候的訪談測試,則會如上述例子一樣地完全公開訊息。

Dialogue 2　延伸對話　 14

It Indeed Is a Warning. 這的確是個警訊。

情境說明 *Situation*

Stuart is the Manager of C Market Research Company, and Owen is the Marketing Manager of N Company. They are talking on the phone about the result from focus group testing for a new perfume.

史都華是 C 市調公司的主管，歐文是 N 公司的行銷經理。他們正在電話上討論新的香水產品所做的焦點團體測試結果。

♀♂ 角色介紹 *Characters*

Stuart: Manager of Market Research Company
Owen: Marketing Manager

史都華：市調公司的主管
歐文：行銷經理

💬 情境對話 *Dialogue*

Stuart: Did you read our analysis report, Owen?

史都華：歐文，你讀過我們的分析結果了嗎？

Owen: Yes, thanks a lot. But there is one question, why our new product got less approvals in each way?

歐文：是的，多謝你們。不過，有個問題。為什麼我們的新產品，在各方面都獲得比較低的認同呢？

1 行銷

2 廣告

3 媒體採購

4 公關公司

5 網路行銷

6 企業社會形象

Stuart: <u>It indeed is a warning</u>. I noticed that, too.

史都華：這的確是個警訊。我也注意到了。

Owen: Oh, My God! The launch time is during next month.

歐文：我的天啊！上市時間就訂在下個月耶。

Stuart: As we suggested on the report, it seems that you have to improve the product and delay the launch time.

史都華：所以如同我們在報告裡建議的一樣，看來只好修改產品並且延遲上市囉。

Owen: Then I have to report to the French headquarter about this problem ASAP. We keep in touch.

歐文：那麼我應該儘快向法國總部反應這個問題。我們保持聯繫。

Stuart: Hey, we should hang out sometime. Like the old saying says: "<u>Don't forget to stop and smell the roses</u>."

史都華：嘿，我們應該找一天聚聚。就像那句諺語說的：「別忘記停下腳步享受生活」。

Owen: <u>You are absolutely right</u>. After the product gets launched, I guess.

歐文：你說得對。就在產品上市之後吧。

短句補給 Useful Phrases

✓ It indeed is a warning. 這的確是個警訊。
✓ Don't forget to stop and smell the roses. 別忘記停下腳步享受生活。
✓ You are absolutely right. 你說得對。

經常有人說：「好的廣告可以帶產品上天堂。」但是要拍出一支好的廣告，也並非易事。拍廣告其實有些小地方值得你我留意，如果你正巧任職在外商廣告公司，或者需要和外國人溝通廣告的細節，那麼你一定不能不知道…。

2.
廣告
Advertising

2-1 主視覺拍攝
Key Visual Shooting

Key visual shooting is a very interesting job but time consuming. If without any character but only shooting the products itself, it would usually take half day to one day. If more characters involve, then it would take at least one full day （i.e. 12 hours）.

　　主視覺的拍攝是個耗時，但是相對有趣的工作。如果只是單純產品拍攝，一般會需要半天至一天拍攝時間，如果拍攝的人物角色越多，則至少會用掉一整天的時間（即十二個小時）。

1 行銷

2 廣告

3 媒體採購

4 公關公司

5 網路行銷

6 企業社會形象

Dialogue 1　主題對話

Retouching Is Needed for That. 那修片是一定要的。

 情境說明 *Situation*

The marketing team has arrived at the studio, as this is the key visual shooting venue for today. The marketing manager is now discussing character gesture with the advertising agency and photographer.

行銷團隊剛剛來到了一個攝影棚，因為這是今天主視覺拍攝的場地。行銷經理現在正與廣告公司、攝影師等一行人討論，關於稍後需要拍攝的人物姿勢。

情境對話 *Dialogue*

Marketing Manager: I would like to have a shot with the model holding the ice cream next to her face. It will be slightly different from the storyboard we confirmed.

行銷經理：我需要一個鏡頭是模特兒拿著冰淇淋，靠在她的臉上。這個鏡頭與我們之前確認過的分鏡腳本稍微有些不同。

Agency: We could add this cut. Since this is a close cut, the food stylist has to continually ensure the ice cream looks non-watery.

廣告公司：我們可以增加這個鏡頭，不過，既然是個近拍，食物造型師得時時注意冰淇淋看起來不會太水。

Photographer: However, the lights in the shooting scene would elevate the temperature. I think we may have to stop shooting every 10 minutes to let the food stylist work on it.

攝影師：但是，在攝影棚裡的燈光會提高室溫，我想我得每隔十分鐘暫停拍攝，讓食物造型師去處理產品。

Agency: Would this effort prolong the shooting time? I only booked the studio until 8pm tonight.

廣告公司：這麼花工夫會不會導致拍攝時間延長？ 我只訂了攝影棚到晚上八點。

Photographer: I am afraid so. We need a total of ten cuts today. The shooting time will be delayed.

攝影師：我想應該會。我們總共需要十個鏡頭，拍攝時間會延誤。

Marketing Manager: Please book the studio until midnight.

行銷經理：請預訂攝影棚的時間到凌晨。

Agency: Okay!

廣告公司：好的！

Photographer: There is another issue I would like to raise. This model's hand is bigger than her face. So the visual image does not look balanced.

攝影師：我還想提出另一個問題，這位模特兒的手，其實比臉大。所以整體視覺上，看起來不太平衡。

Marketing Manager: I see. Could you please use retouching to fix it? Also, the paper cup with the ice cream is not part of the new design we will be using when we launch it next month. Retouching is needed for that as well.

行銷經理：我知道了，能不能請你用電腦修片處理？另外，現在裝冰淇淋用的那個紙杯，其實不會是我們下個月上市時的同樣紙杯，新紙杯有不同的圖案設計，這部分也是需要電腦修片處理。

Agency: No problem. Are we still going to shoot the visual of eating ice cream as the

廣告公司：沒問題。那我們還要拍在腳本中，那張正在

storyboard?

吃冰淇淋的鏡頭嗎？

Marketing Manager: Yes. We need that shot, too.

行銷經理：是的。我們也需要那個鏡頭。

Agency: Then I will have to prepare enough ice cream on side. Every bite needs a newly prepared sample of ice cream.

廣告公司：那我得準備足夠的備品在旁邊，因為每一口拍攝，都需要一個全新處理好造型的冰淇淋。

Photographer: The model is wearing your uniform. Is she your actual employee?

攝影師：那位模特兒穿著你們品牌的制服，請問她是你們真正的員工嗎？

Marketing Manager: She is. She works in one of our branch stores as a part-timer. Speaking of this, did you have her sign the agreement prepared by our legal department?

行銷經理：是的，她在我們一家分店當兼職人員。說到這個，請問你有沒有讓她簽下那份由我們法務部門準備的同意書？

Agency: Yes, you mean the agreement that states she cannot resign from the job until December 31, 2016, and she cannot apply for a job with a competitor for 5 years. She signed it yesterday.

廣告公司：有的。就是那份載明「不可於 2016 年 12 月 31 日前離職，且不可於五年內為競爭品牌工作」的那份同意書？ 她昨天晚上已經簽好了。

ABC 有料字彙 Vocabulary

- **visual** (*n.*) [ˋvɪʒuəl] 主視覺圖
  The key **visual** has much to do with, not only images, but also fonts being used.
  主視覺不只是圖片而已，所用的字型也是重要角色。

- **gesture** (*n.*) [ˋdʒɛstʃɚ] 姿態，手勢
  The important thing for this gathering is to spread the idea and explain what the **gesture** means to all the potential buyers.
  這場聚會最重要的是要對潛在的買家們散播理念並解釋這個姿勢的涵義。

- **storyboard** (*n.*) [ˋstorɪˌbord] 拍片現場的故事腳本
  A good **storyboard** allows you to show what story you have in mind.
  一個好的腳本能呈現你心中的故事。

- **retouch** (*v.*) [riˋtʌtʃ] 潤飾，修片
  They accomplish the effect entirely through digital **retouching**.
  他們完全靠著數位修片達到所要的效果。

- **bite** (*n.*) [baɪt] 一口之量
  Take a **bite** of this. It's delicious!
  吃一口這個。很好吃!

- **character** (*n.*) [ˋkærɪktɚ] 角色，人物
  The five elements of a short story are theme, plot, **characters**, conflict, and setting.
  短篇故事的五個元素就是: 主題、情節、角色、衝突和場景。

- **elevate** (*v.*) [ˋɛləˌvet] 提高，使上昇
  He was **elevated** to the higher position.
  他被升官至更高層級了。

- **prolong** (*v.*) [prəˋlɔŋ] 延長，拖延
  We are trying to figure out some ways to **prolong** the product life circle.
  我們正在想辦法延長產品生命週期。

- **resign** (*v.*) [rɪˋzaɪn] 放棄，辭去
  She **resigned** from that company last month.
  她上個月辭去那家公司職務。

🐤🐤 有料句型 *Sentence Pattern*

句型 1 ↘

A is different from B. A 與 B 是不同的。

It will be slightly **different from** the storyboard we confirmed
那會跟我們確認的腳本有些微的不同。

He is **different from** other boys.
他與其他的男孩不同。

That would be **different from** we thought.
那會與我們原先想的不同。

句型 2 ↘

... is needed. (某)人/事/物是(被)需要的。

Retouching **is needed** for that.
修片是需要的。

An analysis **is needed**.
這需要一份分析。

Plan more budget **is needed**.
規劃多一點費用是必要的。

1 行銷

2 廣告

3 媒體採購

4 公關公司

5 網路行銷

6 企業社會形象

Expert Tips
知識補給

There must be a key visual among a series of product commercials. The images that the key visual is using could be got from an original shot or bought from a image stock, according to how much the budget and the preparation time before the product launches. No matter they are original shots or stock photos, they need to be retouched. An original shot is supposed to satisfy all the demands, such as characters, costumes, and products. Generally speaking, if the budget is sufficient, it will goes to original shots instead of stock photos. There will have less controversies when it comes to the copyright.

　一個系列產品廣告的製作物，一定都有一個主視覺。主視覺所使用的圖片，是完全重新拍攝或是買圖庫公司現成的圖，是依預算與距離上市前的準備時間長短而定，但是不論是全新拍攝的或是買回來的圖，都還是會需要電腦修片。全新拍攝的圖比較可以符合需求，從主角人物的人種、服裝到產品置入在場景中，一般在預算比較充足的情況下，都會採用全新拍攝，並且亦比較不會有版權爭議。

Dialogue 2　延伸對話　16

Tomorrow Is the Commercial Shooting Day.
明天就是廣告拍攝日了。

情境說明 *Situation*

Amy and David are discussing the advertisement contents of a yogurt product for the new season on Skype.

艾咪與大衛正在用 Skype 討論優酪乳商品的新一季廣告拍攝內容。

♀♂角色介紹 *Characters*

Amy: Advertising executives
David: Marketing Manager

艾咪：廣告公司的業務執行
大衛：行銷經理

💬情境對話 *Dialogue*

Amy: Hi, David, tomorrow is the commercial shooting day. There are some details I would like to double check with you.

艾咪：大衛，明天就是拍攝廣告日了。我想和你再次確認細節。

David: Sure. Go ahead.

大衛：沒問題。請說。

Amy: The characters are presented as a

艾咪：廣告主角們是一家

family, which implies that our yogurt is suitable for the whole family.

人，暗示我們的優酪乳全家大小都很適合喝。

David: Yes.

大衛：對。

Amy: Then the shot goes to the father, mother and children separately. <u>The advantages of</u> drinking our yogurt will also be shown on TV.

艾咪：然後鏡頭會分別落在爸爸、媽媽和小朋友身上。電視畫面也會同時秀出他們喝了我們優酪乳的好處。

David: It sounds good.

大衛：聽起來不錯。

Amy: At last, we need to show when and where you can buy it.

艾咪：最後，就是在何時以及到哪裡可以買到。

David: I think we can skip the date since the TV commercial is going to be released one week after the launch date.

大衛：我想還是把上市日期拿掉吧。因為廣告播出時，已經是我們上市一周後了。

Amy: Sure.

艾咪：沒問題。

短句補給 Useful Phrases

✓ I would like to double check with you. 我想與你再次確認。
✓ Go ahead. 說吧！去吧！
✓ The last but not the least,... 最後，但並非不重要的是，…
✓ The Advantage (s) of...is (are)... 的優勢就是…

1 行銷
2 廣告
3 媒體採購
4 公關公司
5 網路行銷
6 企業社會形象

素材租用
Advertising Materials

The material we are adopting is sometimes raw material and sometimes finished material. Regardless of which type it is, the team always needs to do extra work to make it localized.

　　素材的租用分為兩種，有時候是使用乾淨未經處理過的圖，有時候是已經製作完成的廣告物。不管最後是使用哪一種，行銷團隊都還是需要花一番工夫，讓它符合本地的標準，製作成本地市場的廣告物。

1 行銷

2 廣告

3 媒體採購

4 公關公司

5 網路行銷

6 企業社會形象

Dialogue 1　主題對話

Make It Localized! 把素材本土化！

 情境說明 *Situation*

Sometimes and for various reasons, the marketing team might have to use the advertising material developed by a foreign marketing team which is advertising same brand in another country. The manager is now discussing with the specialist the possibility of adopting another country's TVC.

有時候，基於很多原因，行銷部必須使用別的國家同一品牌的行銷團隊，所發展出來的行銷製作物。目前經理正在與自己的團隊討論，使用另一個國家的電視廣告的可能性。

情境對話 *Dialogue*

Sally: I have selected 4 TVCs from the data pool. Those are basically using the same model as the TVCs that we are going to launch.

莎莉：我已經從資料庫中選出四支電視廣告，這幾支電視廣告中，基本上都是使用我們即將上市的同樣型號當主打。

Manager: Yes, but one of them is using a product color that we will not import, meaning we may have to spend considerable money to retouch the color. So, I will skip that one.

經理：對。不過其中有一支廣告是使用我們不會進口的產品顏色，也就是說，我們需要透過電腦修片來處理，這會花更多的費用，因此我會避免使用這一支。

Sally: Right. How about the other three TVCs? I noted that there is one in which the product does not have the small lights on both right and left sides, which happens to violate local government regulations regarding the side light design. So, we either have to retouch it or we cannot use that version.

莎莉：好的。那麼另外三支如何？ 我注意到其中一支廣告所使用的產品，沒有左右側邊小燈的設計，這與本地政府法規不符，因此我們要不是得電腦修片處理，或者也得放棄這個版本。

Manager: Two versions remain on the list of considerations.

經理：那麼只剩下兩個版本，是我們還可以考慮的。

Tom: I have checked with branch offices about those two versions, and one is a Japan production and another is a German production. The German version royalty cost is higher than the one from Japan.

湯姆：我查過關於這兩個版本的分公司，一個是日本的版本，另一個是德國的版本。德國的版權費用要比日本的版權費用來得高。

Manager: But I would rather use the German version because our key success factor and unique selling point is "origin and imported". If we use the Japanese version, then all the actors in TVC will be Asian. The audiences will not relate to "imported" directly.

經理：但是我寧用使用德國的版本，因為我們的關鍵成功因素是『原創與原裝』，如果我們使用日本版本，那麼所有電視廣告中的演員們都會是亞洲面孔，觀眾也因此無法直接感受到「原裝」的這個點。

Sally: I endorse this point.

莎莉：我也同意這個看法。

1 行銷

2 廣告

3 媒體採購

4 公關公司

5 網路行銷

6 企業社會形象

Tom: The German marketing team insists that the video file not be released until the remittance for the copyright has been paid. I will talk to our accounting to process ASAP.

湯姆：德國的行銷團隊堅持要等到收到我們完成版權使用的匯款後，才會釋出影片的檔案，我會儘快請會計開始這些程序。

Manager: There is another issue. One scene in that TVC shows other models that we will not launch in the Taiwan market. We will have to cut it out, and reshoot another 5 seconds to replace it. Plus, can we use the final cut as our KV for POSM?

經理：這裡還有另一個問題，在電視廣告裡面其中有一幕，出現了其他幾種型號是我們不會在台灣市場上市的產品，我們需要把這一幕剪掉，並重拍五秒的畫面，補進這支廣告中。對了，我們可以用最後一幕停格的畫面，當成我們平面製作物的主視覺？

Sally: I think so. It is a perfect cut. So we could save the whole shooting budget and budget for creating the KV.

莎莉：我也覺得可以，那是個很棒的畫面。這樣一來我們還可以省下，原本整個平面製作物主視覺的拍攝與設計費用。

Tom: How about the copyright royalty, the music copyright does not belong to our German branch office but rather to a music house in Europe. I have to contact them tomorrow to make sure we can use it here in Taiwan.

湯姆：關於版權費用，音樂版權的部分不屬於我們德國的分公司，而是另一家在歐洲的音樂工作室，我明天還得與他們聯繫，確認一下我們能不能在台灣使用這段音樂。

Manager: It's not a big problem. I suggest that we should change the background music, because the original music is now out of date. It would lead the audience to believe that this TVC is not a new production.

經理：這不是大問題，我建議我們應該換掉背景音樂，因為原本的音樂已經有一點過時，會讓觀眾很容易發現，這支電視廣告不是一支新廣告。

Sally: Then I will let the advertising company find the replace music, and the music has to be on trend.

莎莉：那麼我會請廣告公司找一段可以適合且正在流行的音樂，重新配進電視廣告裡。

ABC 有料字彙 Vocabulary

- **regardless** (*adv.*) [rɪˋgɑrdlɪs] 不管…
  He decides to go the other way **regardless** of the previous agreement.
  他打算不管先前的協議，採取另一種做法。

- **localize** (*v.*) [ˋlok!͵aɪz] 在地化
  The marketing strategy needs to be **localized** even for a global enterprise.
  即使是跨國企業，行銷策略也有在地化的需要。

- **various** (*a.*) [ˋvɛrɪəs] 各種的，形形色色的
  There are **various** colors and styles for customers to choose.
  有各式各樣的顏色及款式可供顧客選擇。

1 行銷

2 廣告

3 媒體採購

4 公關公司

5 網路行銷

6 企業社會形象

- **considerable** (*a.*) [kən`sɪdərəb!] 相當多的
  They successfully introduce a new product into the market beyond the **considerable** language barrier.
  他們超越相當大的語言障礙，成功將新產品引進市場。

- **violate** (*v.*) [`vaɪəˌlet] 違反，違犯
  Be careful not to **violate** the morality and ethics when seeking creativity and innovation.
  追求創意與創新時，小心不要違犯了道德倫理。

- **regulation** (*n.*) [ˌrɛgjə`leʃən] 法規，條例
  This product became well-known because it broke the local government **regulations**.
  這產品因為違反當地政府法規而變得廣為人知。

- **endorse** (*v.*) [ɪn`dɔrs] 附和，認同
  Many celebrities **endorse** the product.
  很多名人認同這產品。

- **remittance** (*n.*) [rɪ`mɪtns] 電匯，匯款
  You may make a payment by **remittance**.
  您可以電匯付款。

- **copyright** (*n.*) [`kɑpɪˌraɪt] 版權
  Make sure you own the **copyright** before you upload anything.
  上傳任何東西之前，請確定你擁有它的版權。

- **out of date** 已過時的
  This is not **out of date**. It's the remembrance of the past.
  這不是過時。這是對過去的紀念。

🐤🐤 有料句型 *Sentence Pattern*

句型 1 ↘

either A or B　不是 A 就是 B

We **either** have to retouch it **or** we cannot use that version.
我們要不就是修片，要不就是不用那個版本。

You can **either** stay **or** leave.
你可以留下或自行離開。

I think I will **either** sell it **or** give it away.
我想我會賣掉或送給別人。

句型 2 ↘

not (only)... but rather...　不但…，反而…。

The music copyright does **not** belong to our German branch office **but rather** to a music house.
這音樂版權不屬於我們的德國分公司，而是屬於一家音樂工作室。

The patient was **not** better **but rather** grew worse.
病人不但沒變好，反而更惡化了。

You should **not** consider if they can come or not **but rather** if they want to.
你不該考慮他們是否能來，而是該想想是否他們願意來。

Expert Tips
知識補給

If the key visual is not original shots, the images used in commercials will be retrieved from a image stock gallery, called buying/renting stock images. For example, it is royalty-free or other license rights, for how much and for how long, used in what media? Those have very much to do with the fee. Moreover, the retouching is needed more for those photos from a image stock, for example, when you need to add the brand logo on the these photos. This won't be a problem for a whole new original shot.

如果主視覺並非全新拍攝，則會需要向圖庫公司租圖，一般稱為租素材。通常這樣的情況比較容易有版權的問題，比如買下的使用版權是買斷，使用一年或以上，且使用在什麼媒體上，都與租用版費用息息相關。此外，租用的圖通常需要修圖的部分會比全新拍攝多，比如說：得將 Logo 與產品修圖置入，這是全新拍攝的視覺不會遇到的問題。

Dialogue 2　延伸對話　💿18 ▶

Pay Attention to Contract and Quotation. 留意合約與報價單

☕ **情境說明** *Situation*

Olivia and Norm are discussing the division of work between two departments during the commercial shooting period.

奧莉薇亞正和諾姆討論著在新產品廣告拍攝期間，兩部門間的分工項目。

♀♂ **角色介紹** *Characters*

Olivia: Product Manager
Norm: Marketing Manager

奧莉薇亞：產品經理
諾姆：行銷經理

💬 **情境對話** *Dialogue*

Olivia: Right, Norm, I would like to confirm with you is there anything our department can help with?

奧莉薇亞：對了，諾姆，我想和你確認一下還有什麼需要我們部門幫忙的？

Norm: There is a small problem and I hope there is someone in your department that can help.

諾姆：有個小問題，但願你們部門有人可以幫忙。

Olivia: Sure, what is that?

奧莉薇亞：請說。

Norm: It's about a key visual which we are going to published on a magazine. We probably need to buy it from A Company.

諾姆：是關於要刊登在雜誌上的一個主視覺。可能要和 A 公司去購買照片。

Olivia: Oh? Do you have the number of the contact person?

奧莉薇亞：哦？有沒有那位聯絡人電話？

Norm: Yes, I do. There it is.

諾姆：有的，在這裡。

Olivia: This is my first time to deal with this kind of thing, is there anything I should pay attention to?

奧莉薇亞：因為我是第一次處理這種事情，有沒有什麼我應該注意的地方？

Norm: Don't worry about it. I will check the contract and quotation for you then.

諾姆：別擔心。合約和報價單屆時我會幫忙留意。

短句補給 Useful Phrases

✓ Is there anything I can help with?　有沒有什麼是我可以幫忙的？
✓ There it is.　在這裡。
✓ Don't worry about it.　別擔心。

105

廣告物製作
POSM

POSM, point of sales material, is a term used when talking about advertising printed materials. The job for the marketing specialist is to negotiate the most efficient quantity and cost. Printing 10 posters sometimes is exactly the same price as printing 80 copies.

POSM 廣告製作物，顧名思義即為幫助銷售的物品。一個稱職的行銷專員，需要了解每樣製作物的最佳經濟量，因為有時候印刷十張海報與印製八十張是完全一樣的價錢。

1 行銷

2 廣告

3 媒體採購

4 公關公司

5 網路行銷

6 企業社會形象

Dialogue 1　主題對話

Printing 10 Posters Sometimes Is Exactly the Same Price As Printing 80 Copies. 印十張海報有時跟印八十張價錢是一樣的。

 情境說明 *Situation*

The advertising agency usually has an art director to control all the design and printing quality. <u>The art director is paying a visit to the client</u> to show the mock-up of all printed materials today.

通常廣告公司都會有一個藝術總監掌控所有的設計與製作物的品質，今天藝術總監正前往客戶的辦公室，準備提交所有製作物的打樣。

情境對話 *Dialogue*

Marketing Specialist: The art director and his team from the advertising agency are here. They are going to present the mock-up for the poster, banner, window sticker, flyer, tray mat, coupon, standee and mailer.

行銷專員：廣告公司的創意總監與他的同事都已經到了，他們今天要提案所有製作物的打樣，包括海報、橫幅旗幟、窗貼、傳單、餐墊紙、折價券、立牌與郵寄廣告。

Marketing Manager: Sure. As I know the lead-time is very short. So since they didn't have time earlier to propose the designs for all materials separately, I guess then we have to confirm both the design and mock-up all together today. Right?

行銷經理：當然，我知道整個案子的執行時間太短，所以他們沒有時間事先提案每一個製作物個別的設計，我猜想今天我們得一次確認設計與打樣的質感顏色，是吧？

Art Director: Exactly. So, shall we start from the banner, tray mat and coupon?

創意總監：確實如此，所以我們先從橫幅旗幟、餐墊紙與折價券看起，好嗎？

Marketing Manager: Okay.

行銷經理：沒問題。

Art Director: The confirmed KV (key visual) is horizontal design, and so is the banner, tray mat and coupon. Therefore, I think there will be less potential problems.

創意總監：由於已確認的主視覺是橫式設計，而橫幅旗幟、餐墊紙與折價券也是橫式設計，所以我想會衍生出來的問題比較少。

Marketing Specialist: I have done the proof-reading of all wording, including the legal protection terms and conditions.

行銷專員：我已經校正過所有的內容文字，包括法律保護文字。

Marketing Manager: It looks good. But I think the blank space between the logo and cutting edge should tally with the logo guidelines. Also, according to the logo guidelines, our logo could be used as standard green, blue, black and white. I don't think we are allowed to use red?

行銷經理：看起來很不錯，但是我想 logo 與切紙邊緣需要留白的距離，需要和使用標準裡所規定一致，此外，依照 logo 使用標準裡的規定，我們的 logo 可以使用標準色的綠，其他如藍、黑和白也都可以使用，但是我不認為我們可以使用紅色。

Art Director: I understand, however, this happens to be a Chinese New Year promotion. Using red shows more Chinese holiday ambience.

創意總監：我了解，但是因為是中國農曆年期間的促銷，使用紅色會比較有節慶的氣氛。

1 行銷

2 廣告

3 媒體採購

4 公關公司

5 網路行銷

6 企業社會形象

Marketing Manager: Yes, then I will have to send the design to the head office in the U.S. to seek for special design approval. I don't think we have time to go through this process.

行銷經理：對，但是如此一來，這變成了特殊設計，我還得寄到在美國的總公司去審核，我不認為我們有足夠的時間進行這樣的程序。

Art Director: <u>In that case, then I will use red as the background color</u> and keep the logo as white.

創意總監：這樣的話，那麼我會用紅色當底色，讓 logo 還是使用反白色。

Marketing Manager: Please do so.

行銷經理：請這麼改。

Art Director: Here are the posters, flyers, stickers, standees and mailers. They are all vertical designs.

創意總監：這裡是海報、傳單、窗貼、立牌與郵寄廣告，這些都是直式的設計。

Marketing Manager: The product has been switched the side. It's fine. Yet the font on standee is not the standard font. We use Cambria font for content wording.

行銷經理：產品被調換了邊，這沒關係。不過，在立牌上的字體，不是我們規定的標準字體，我們一向都是使用正黑體當內文的字體。

Art Director: I will revise that. How about the sticker?

創意總監：這部分我會改，窗貼看起來如何？

Marketing Manager: I think all product pictures have to employ the same standard of colors. The bread on the poster is a little too yellow compared to the bread on

行銷經理：我想所有的製作物圖片，應該要在顏色上都維持同一標準，海報上的麵包比立牌上的麵包還黃，窗

standee, yet the tomato on the sticker is too orange compared to the poster. Also, the potato color is not consistent either. I understand that even using the same color of ink to print would nevertheless yield different results due to the differences in materials. I think that is your job to control the quality.

Art Director: I agree. I will try to deal with this issue. On the other hand, I suggest that we should use retouching to trim the lettuce, as the real product does not have so much lettuce.

Marketing Manager: Yes. That would help avoid any consumer complaints.

貼上的番茄也比海報上的更橘，然而，馬鈴薯的顏色在個製作物上都不一致，我了解在不同的材質上印刷，即便使用同樣一色號的印刷色，印出來的成果不會完全一致，但是掌控好品質，應該是你們的工作。

創意總監：我同意，我會去克服這個問題。不過另一方面，我建議我們應該電腦修片一下生菜的部分，讓它看起來少一點，因為真正的產品裡生菜沒有這麼多。

行銷經理：好的，這樣一來也可以避免消費者投訴產品不實。

ABC 有料字彙 Vocabulary

- **mock-up** (n.) [mɑkʌp] 打樣，模型
  We can see a **mock-up** of the whole Taipei 101 building at the show.
  我們可以在那場活動中看到整棟台北 101 建築的實體模型。

- **lead time** 作業時間
  As far as this case is concerned, we tend to sign long-term

contracts with at least six months **lead time**.

以這個案子來看，我們傾向簽長約，前置作業期間至少六個月。

- **horizontal** (*a.*) [ˌhɑrəˋzɑnt!] 水平的，橫式的
  I want these flags to be placed in a **horizontal** position.
  我要這些旗幟以橫向擺放。

- **terms and conditions** 法律文字
  You should read those **terms and conditions** thoroughly.
  你應該仔細徹底地讀那些條款。

- **ambience** (*n.*) [ˋæmbɪəns] 氣氛，情調
  We are looking for a restaurant with a romantic **ambience**.
  我們正在找一家有浪漫情調的餐廳。

- **vertical** (*a.*) [ˋvɝtɪk!] 垂直的，直式的
  These giveaways are going to be wrapped in a box with **vertical** stripes.
  這些贈品將被裝在直條圖案的盒子裡。

- **nevertheless** (*adv.*) [ˌnɛvɚðəˋlɛs] 不過，但是
  The location is good. **Nevertheless**, we still need a good discount.
  這地點不錯。不過我們還是需要一個好折扣。

- **yield** (*v.*) [jild] 產生，衍生
  The entire endeavors for the past years **yield** fruitful results.
  過去幾年的努力有了豐收的結果。

- **trim** (*v.*) [trɪm] 修剪，縮減
  The marketing budgets **trimmed** back considerably.
  行銷預算大幅地縮減。

1 行銷

2 廣告

3 媒體採購

4 公關公司

5 網路行銷

6 企業社會形象

有料句型 *Sentence Pattern*

句型 1 ↘

pay a visit to...　去拜訪...

The art director **is paying a visit to** the client.
藝術總監正在拜訪客戶。

I would like to **pay a visit to** that company.
我想去拜訪那間公司。

Do you mind to **pay a visit to** his office tomorrow?
你介不介意明天到他辦公室一趟？

句型 2 ↘

In that case,...　（若是）那樣的話…

In that case, then I will use red as the background color.
那樣的話，我會用紅色做為背景顏色。

In that case, I suggest you don't go.
那樣的話，我建議你不要去。

In that case, you should really help him.
如果是那樣的話，你真的應該幫他。

1 行銷

2 廣告

3 媒體採購

4 公關公司

5 網路行銷

6 企業社會形象

Expert Tips
知識補給

There is some standard rules for each brand. If the commercial company has been working with the brand for a period of time, it should be familiar with all the relevant rules in order to avoid mistakes. However, if it is a new partner, you need to repeatedly urge it and pay more attention when you proofread all the materials. Besides, after the key visual is confirmed, the commercial company will develop the other promotional production according to the key visual.

　　每一個品牌都有 logo 使用的標準規則，一般如果與廣告公司合作已久，該公司便會熟讀所有的相關使用規定，避免發生錯誤，但是如果是剛合作不久的廣告公司，則需要叮嚀許久並且在校稿時多留意，此外，通常主視覺的設計被確認後，廣告公司就會依照主視覺來發展所有其他製作物。

Dialogue 2 　延伸對話　　　　　◎20

We'd Better Put a Warning Here. 我們最好在這裡加註警語。

 情境說明 *Situation*

Al and George are colleagues at Marketing Department, and they are talking about the schedule of POSM.

艾爾與喬治是行銷部的同事，他們正在談論廣告製作物的進度。

♀♂角色介紹 *Characters*

Al: Marketing Specialist
George: Marketing Specialist

艾爾：行銷專員
喬治：行銷專員

 情境對話 *Dialogue*

Al: George, I think the schedule of this POSM has some problems.

艾爾：喬治，我想這張廣告製作物的進度表有點問題。

George: How come?

喬治：怎麼説呢？

Al: Usually we provide it to the Manager six months prior, and then she will review it and tell us where to adjust.

艾爾：通常是六個月前要提供給主管過目，然後她會審核並告訴我們要修改的地方。

George: Oh, no, the commercial will be

喬治：糟糕，廣告是八月要

launched on TV in August and now is May.

開始在電視上播放，而現在已經是五月了。

Al: You are right. You should be more careful about it. And…

艾爾：對呀。你應該更用心一點。還有…

George: Any other problems?

喬治：還有問題嗎？

Al: Yes. We'd better put a warning here, says" The Company may change, remove, cancel, or otherwise modify the event at any time without prior notice".

艾爾：有。這裡最好加註警語：本公司保留隨時修改、變更或取消活動之權利並可不事先告知。

George: Thank you so much! I'll get right on it!

喬治：真是太感激你了！我馬上處理！

短句補給 Useful Phrases

✓ I think…has some problems. 我想…有點問題。
✓ Any other problems? 還有問題嗎？
✓ I'll get right on it. 我馬上處理！

在日常生活當中，都不可避免地會接觸到媒體。臉書、名人部落格、電視、雜誌、報紙、廣播、戶外看板…等等，在在都是一種媒體或資訊傳播的媒介，其重要性不言可喻。行銷人對於媒體採購有哪些注意事項，也不可不知。

3.
媒體採購
Media Buy

媒體計劃
Media Plan

Rookie
菜鳥心聲

The media plan seems very easy to prepare, just make sure which portion of which type of media. But there are a lot of small details that we have to look into it. It usually will discuss together with the media buying plan.

媒體計劃看似簡單，通常只要準備好分配哪些類型的媒體需要多少的預算。但是其實還是有很多細節是得注意的，一般來說，媒體計劃會與媒體採購的會議一起進行。

1 行銷

2 廣告

3 媒體採購

4 公關公司

5 網路行銷

6 企業社會形象

Dialogue 1　主題對話　21

It's All about the Budget！一切都是預算的關係！

 情境說明 *Situation*

The media buyer is discussing with the marketing manager about how to allocate the limited budget and maximize the effect.

媒體採購正在與行銷經理討論，如何將有限的預算，進行最有效用的分配。

情境對話 *Dialogue*

Marketing Manager: About this project, with limited budget, I think we cannot do TVC, but can do print media, news placement and outdoor banner.

行銷經理：關於這個計劃，在有限的預算下，我想我們不能上電視廣告。但是應該可以上平面媒體、新聞置入，以及戶外廣告。

Buyer: Understood. About the print media, do you mean we just plan the newspaper only?

媒體採購：了解，關於平面廣告，您是指報紙而已嗎？

Marketing Manager: Yes, as people don't read magazine nowadays. Besides, I think with our budget, we can only do one newspaper.

行銷經理：是的，現在大多數的人已經不讀雜誌了。此外，我想我們的預算也只夠上報紙廣告而已。

Buyer: I see. Then we will plan 30% for

媒體採購：這樣啊，那麼我

print media and 40% for outdoor banner and the rest for news placement.

們會規劃百分之三十上平面媒體，百分之四十上戶外看版，剩下的安排新聞置入。

Marketing Manager: How many front-page ads on the newspaper you think we could purchase with that budget?

行銷經理：請問你想，我們能購買得了幾檔報紙首頁的廣告呢？

Buyer: I think only 2 front-page ads on weekdays.

媒體採購：我想應該只有在平日時段，兩檔首頁廣告。

Marketing Manager: That's really not enough. Can you please get more free pages for us? We brought lots newspaper ads in the past.

行銷經理：這樣真的不夠。請問你可以要到多幾檔免費的廣告嗎？我們過去買了很多報紙廣告的。

Buyer: The sales representative from that newspaper actually contacted me a few days ago talking about one free page. I will see what I can do.

媒體採購：那家報紙的業務代表其實前幾天有和我聯絡，有聊到免費的版面。我來試試看能夠要到多少。

Marketing Manager: Great! About the news placement, can we do one-time placement on the channel W?

行銷經理：太好了！關於新聞置入，我們能夠在 W 頻道做一次性的置入嗎？

Buyer: Well, I don't think it's a possible. That channel basically do not accept one-time news placement. Their package is

媒體採購：我想應該不可能。那個頻道基本上不接受一次性的新聞置入，他們的

three-time placement, plus one extra placement in the entertainment talking show. The package is fixed and costly.

組合是三次新聞置入，外加一次娛樂談話性節目的置入，這個組合價位相當高且不可變更條件。

Marketing Manager: I see. If so, then please try the channel S.

行銷經理：知道了。如果這樣的話，請試試看 S 頻道。

Buyer: Sure.

媒體採購：好的。

Marketing Manager: Concerning the outdoor banner, I would like to book the one on the intersection of XX road and QQ road.

行銷經理：關於戶外看板，我想買位於 XX 路與 QQ 路十字路口的那個看板。

Buyer: That one is very popular. Usually you have to book it 3 months ahead.

媒體採購：那個看板相當熱門，通常在三個月前都會被訂滿。

Marketing Manager: How about another one on TT road?

行銷經理：那麼在 TT 路上的那個看板呢？

Buyer: That one is an LCD outdoor banner. So we are planning to play the TVC on it?

媒體採購：那個看板是個液晶看板，所以我們要用它來播放電視廣告嗎？

Marketing Manager: Yes. We could use last

行銷經理：是的，我們可以

1 行銷
2 廣告
3 媒體採購
4 公關公司
5 網路行銷
6 企業社會形象

year TVC to play on that banner.

用去年製作的那支電視廣告。

Buyer: Just a reminder that LCD banner usually plays some inappropriate TVCs of local brands. Do you really want to let our brand associate with those brands?

媒體採購：只是一個小提醒，那個液晶看板平時都播放一些不太妥當的本土品牌電視廣告，你確定要讓我們的品牌和那些品牌連結在一起嗎？

Marketing Manager: Well, thank you for your reminder. Is there any other banner that you have in mind?

行銷經理：這樣啊，謝謝你的提醒。有沒有其他的看板，你現在想得到的？

Buyer: I will go back to check the schedule and let you know later today.

媒體採購：我會回去看一下預定的時間表，今天晚一點再告訴您。

ABC 有料字彙 Vocabulary

- **placement** (*n.*) [ˋplɛsmənt] 置入
  Let me give you more examples of product **placement**!
  讓我舉更多有關產品置入的例子吧!

- **weekday** (*n.*) [ˋwikˏde] 平日，工作日
  These performances are always on **weekdays,** sometimes on weekends.
  這些表演總是在平日演出，有時在週末。

- **representative** (*n.*) [ˌrɛprɪˋzɛntətɪv] 代表，代理人
  She has been the **representative** of the company for many years.
  她已經好幾年都是那家公司的代表了。

- **entertainment** (*n.*) [ˌɛntɚˋtenmənt] 娛樂，演藝
  This time we will target at adult **entertainment** business.
  這一次我們要瞄準成人娛樂事業。

- **concerning** (*prep.*) [kənˋsɝnɪŋ] 關於
  Our staff in the consumer services division can help with issues **concerning** refunds.
  我們在消費者服務部門的人員能處理有關退款之事宜。

- **intersection** (*n.*) [ˌɪntɚˋsɛkʃən] 十字路口
  The show is held at the **intersection** of two highways.
  這場秀在兩條公路交界處舉行。

- **inappropriate** (*a.*) [ˌɪnəˋproprɪɪt] 不恰當的
  It is **inappropriate** to talk behind people's back.
  在人後說長道短是不恰當的。

- **associate** (*v.*) [əˋsoʃɪɪt] 使關聯
  I don't want the customers **associate** my brand with the other.
  我不想要客戶把我的品牌和另一個品牌做關聯。

- **reminder** (*n.*) [rɪˋmaɪndɚ] 提醒，提示
  The news is a **reminder** that "fish follow the bait."
  這則新聞是個提醒：「貪小便宜等著上當受騙」。

- **maximize** (*v.*) [ˋmæksəˌmaɪz] 使增加到最大限度
  The priority for our company this year to **maximize** the profit.
  公司今年的首要目標就是利潤最大化。

123

🐤🐤 有料句型 Sentence Pattern

句型 1 ↘

have in mind　心中有想法

Is there any other banner that you **have in mind**?
妳心中有其它關於橫幅的想法嗎？

What do you **have in mind**?
你有什麼想法？

What kind of starting pay do you **have in mind**?
你希望起薪多少？

句型 2 ↘

to associate A with B　將 A 與 B 做連結

Do you really want to let our brand **associate with** those brands?
你真的想要讓我們的品牌跟那些品牌有關係嗎？

We naturally **associate** the name of Darwin **with** the doctrine of evolution.
我們很自然地將達爾文與進化論連結在一起。

Never **associate with** bad companions.
永遠別交壞朋友。

Expert Tips
知識補給

Basically, the media plan depends on the budget you have. Maximize the effect with limited budget is the key. Sometime when the budget is tight, we could negotiate with the media buying agency for extra free exposures.

基本上，所有的媒體計劃都得視預算的多寡來安排。儘量在有限預算內，放大媒體曝光量。有的時候當預算相當緊的時候，我們也可以和媒體採購公司談判，以他們平日與媒體的關係，多爭取到一些免費的版位或媒體曝光。

Dialogue 2　延伸對話　◎22

Where to Announce The Advertisements? 應該在哪裡刊登廣告？

 情境說明 *Situation*

Fiona and Gary are talking about where to advertise of their new online game.

費歐娜和蓋瑞正在討論公司的線上遊戲商品，應該在哪裡刊登廣告。

♀♂ **角色介紹** *Characters*

Fiona: Product Manager
Gary: Advertising Specialist

費歐娜：產品經理
蓋瑞：廣告專員

 情境對話 *Dialogue*

Fiona: Gary, how nice to see you here, could you do me a favor?

費歐娜：蓋瑞，在這遇見你真好，願意幫我一個忙嗎？

Gary: Of course. How can I help?

蓋瑞：當然。我能幫您什麼呢？

Fiona: I listed a media list of where to put the new online game's advertisements, and maybe you can discuss with your Manager?

費歐娜：我列了一份新的遊戲產品應該在哪些媒體刊登廣告，或許你可以和部門主管討論一下？

Gary: <u>I would love to!</u> Well, I think I may have a small suggestion for this list.

蓋瑞：我很樂意！嗯，我想我對這份名單有些小建議。

Fiona: Really? Please.

費歐娜：哦？請說。

Gary: I suggest we replace the radio advertising with the "viral marketing" through online game players.

蓋瑞：我建議刪掉電台廣告，改為線上遊戲玩家的「病毒式行銷」。

Fiona: Good idea, but will that cheaper than radio advertising?

費歐娜：好主意，但是比電台廣告還便宜嗎？

Gary: Basically, yes. I will give you a list of expenses.

蓋瑞：基本上是的。我晚一點列張費用單給您。

Fiona: <u>That would be great!</u>

費歐娜：太棒了！

短句補給 Useful Phrases

✓ Could you do me a favor? 能幫我一個忙嗎？
✓ I would love to. 我很樂意。
✓ That would be great! 太棒了！

1 行銷
2 廣告
3 媒體採購
4 公關公司
5 網路行銷
6 企業社會形象

3-2 採購與評估
Media Buying & Evaluation

The media buying usually would be dealt thru an agency. We depend on the agency suggestion a lot, and yet we also aware that the agency occasionally intends to sell some media which its performance is not well. We have to be very careful not to waste the budget.

　　媒體採購通常都是透過媒體採購公司。雖然仰賴採購公司給我們的建議，但是我們也很明白採購公司有時候會要我們買一些表現不好的媒體。得小心避免浪費媒體購買的預算。

1 行銷
2 廣告
3 媒體採購
4 公關公司
5 網路行銷
6 企業社會形象

Dialogue 1　主題對話

It's Not Really Driving Product Sales.
其實那並不見得會有助於產品銷售。

 情境說明 *Situation*

The media buyers are having a meeting with the marketing team. The team is about to debrief to the media buyer about the new project.

媒體採購同仁正與行銷團隊開會中，行銷部正要提出一個新案子的媒體採購需求。

情境對話 *Dialogue*

Buyer: What is target and scope of the project?

媒體採購：請問這個案的目標與範圍大致是如何？

Marketing Manager: TVC is our main material. The target is 500 GRP for 3 weeks. Since the weight of exposures is limited, please focus on prime time and the programs with high rating target audiences (TAs).

行銷經理：電視廣告是我們主要的素材，目標是三週內達到 500 收視點。由於此次的下的採購量不是很大（媒體採購都稱「下廣告」），因此請著重在黃金時段與那些我們主要消費群所收看的高收視節目。

Buyer: What is the TA behavior?

媒體採購：請問主要消費群的行為模式為何？

Marketing Manager: Age 20 to 34. Male

行銷經理：年齡 20 至 34

based, love to seek for new adventure.

歲，男性為主，喜好探索新的事物。

Buyer: I see. I think movie and news channels should be invested heavier.

媒體採購：瞭解，我建議可以加重在電影頻道與新聞頻道的投放。

Marketing Manager: Could you share with me the most up-to-date news channel ratio data?

行銷經理：請問可以提供一下最新的新聞頻道視聽比例數據嗎？

Buyer: Sure, I will send it to you later. And yet, the news channel audience gender percentage is 55% male versus 45% female as I recall.

媒體採購：當然可以，我稍後會寄給您。然而就我的印象中，新聞頻道的收看對象男性佔百分之 55，女性為百分之 45。

Marketing Manager: Except the TVC, also we need outdoor board and digital media exposures.

行銷經理：除了電視廣告，我們仍需要戶外看板與網路媒體的曝光。

Buyer: Would we have an event site created for the product launch?

媒體採購：請問產品上市時，我們會開設一個活動網頁嗎？

Marketing Manager: Yes, we will develop an online event to interact with consumers.

行銷經理：會的。我們會開設一個活動網站和消費者互動。

Buyer: So we would also need to invest some Internet banners on Yahoo and Youtube to attract people visiting the event site.

媒體採購：那麼在搜尋網站如 Yahoo 和 Youtube 首頁的看板式廣告也是需要的，以便將消費者導入活動網頁。

1 行銷
2 廣告
3 媒體採購
4 公關公司
5 網路行銷
6 企業社會形象

Marketing Manager: Correct. We need to hire some social media influencers to create the Buzz and WOM (Word-of-Mouth) effect as well.

行銷經理：沒錯。也需要找一些意見領袖在社群網站上發表一些文章，創造一些話題。

Buyer: Do we need to re-edit the TVC?

媒體採購：請問電視廣告的長度是否需要重新剪輯？

Marketing Manager: The current version is standard 35″, you may need to create a 25″ version.

行銷經理：目前的長度為標準版 35 秒，應該需要剪接一版為 25 秒。

Buyer: Can you please share with me the launch plan and budget allocation after the meeting?

媒體採購：請問可以會議結束，提供給我此次產品上市計畫與預算分配？

Marketing Manager: Of course. I hope you can manage to make the average frequency of TVC to 4 times.

行銷經理：當然可以。我期望這次的媒體採購分配可以讓電視廣告重覆收看數字達到四次。

Buyer: What would be the GRP allocation of weekday and weekend?

媒體採購：請問收視點的分配是該集中在平日或週末？

Marketing Manager: I would like to hear your idea after consideration.

行銷經理：這部份我想聽聽你們評估後的想法。

Buyer: Noted. I will send you the media buy plan by COB this upcoming Friday. And we could have further discussion over the phone.

媒體採購：瞭解。那麼我們會在本週五下班前，將媒體採購計畫書寄過來，之後再以電話溝通與進一步的討論。

131

ABC 有料字彙 Vocabulary

- **scope** (*n.*) [skop] 範圍，領域
  We need to define the **scope** of this investigation.
  我們需要先定義調查的範圍。

- **exposure** (*n.*) [ɪkˋspoʒɚ] 曝光，揭露
  I have plenty of low-cost tips to get **exposure** for your brand.
  我有一堆低成本的訣竅來曝光你的品牌。

- **adventure** (*n.*) [ədˋvɛntʃɚ] 冒險活動或經歷
  Now it's time to start the **adventure** with us.
  現在，和我們一起展開冒險的時間到了。

- **gender** (*n.*) [ˋdʒɛndɚ] 性別
  Is there a **gender** gap in the design industry?
  在設計產業中是否有性別上的差距呢?

- **influencer** (*n.*) [ˋɪnflʊənsɚ] 有影響力的人
  Those who are being called "**influencers**" are our targets, and
  what we are doing now is called "Influencer Marketing."
  那些被稱為「有影響力的人」正是我們的目標，而我們所正在做的稱為「影響者
  行銷」。

- **frequency** (*n.*) [ˋfrikwənsɪ] 頻率，次數
  The behavior of placing an order is happening with increasing
  frequency.
  下單行為發生的頻率持續增加中。

- **allocation** (*n.*) [ˌæləˋkeʃən] 分派，配置
  You are in charge of the **allocation** of all the resources.
  你是主導所有資源配置的人。

- **occasionally** (*adv.*) [əˋkeʒənlɪ] 偶爾，有時
  Occasionally I stop putting a smile on my face.
  偶爾我會停止微笑。

- **ratio** (*n.*) [ˋreʃo] 比例
  The **ratio** of guests to waiters is 6:1.
  顧客與服務生的比例是六比一。

- **TVC** = TV commercial
  電視廣告

- **GRP** = Gross Rating Point
  收視點

- **COB** = close of business
  當日下班前

- **Buzz** = 話題、流行熱度

1 行銷

2 廣告

3 媒體採購

4 公關公司

5 網路行銷

6 企業社會形象

🐤🐤 有料句型 Sentence Pattern

句型 1 ↘

manage to V 想辦法…

I hope you can **manage to** make the average frequency of TVC to 4 times.

我希望你能想辦法可以讓電視廣告重覆收看數字達到四次。

She **managed to** finish all the work.

她想出辦法來完成所有工作。

We finally **managed to** get there in time.

我們最後及時趕到。

句型 2 ↘

over the phone 透過電話

We could have further discussion **over the phone**.

我們可以透過電話做更多討論。

I can't tell you **over the phone**.

我不能用電話告訴你。

My mom is talking with her friend **over the phone**.

我媽正在用電話和朋友聊天。

1 行銷

2 廣告

3 媒體採購

4 公關公司

5 網路行銷

6 企業社會形象

Expert Tips
知識補給

You have to well understand not only your products but also your objective, target (audiences) when you briefing to the agency. So that media buy agency could fully understand your needs. Sometimes the media buy agency would try to sell you the media which is close / friendly to them yet is not really benefit to drive product sales. So to check the general media rating is very important.

　　在與媒體採購公司簡報前，除了對產品要非常熟悉，也應該要非常瞭解溝通重點、目標（的對象），清楚讓媒體採購公司知道該向那些人溝通且要説什麼話，才能協調與安排出一份較有效用的媒體採購計畫。此外，有時候媒體採購公司會試著説服你在一些奇怪的媒體/時段下廣告，那只是因為該媒體與採購公司之間有些特殊默契，花了錢卻不一定對產品銷售有任何幫助，因此要熟悉各媒體與節目的收視評比是很重要的。

Dialogue 2　延伸對話 24

If It Doesn't Work Out, We Can Change to Others.
如果沒有效果的話，我們可以改成其他媒體。

🍵 情境說明 *Situation*

Ruth and Emily are discussing their group project, which is "Where a new handbag should be advertised."

露絲與艾蜜莉正在討論她們的小組關於「新上市的手提包應該在哪裡投放廣告？」的小組報告。

♀♂ 角色介紹 *Characters*

Ruth: Student in Marketing Department
Emily: Student in Marketing Department

露絲：行銷系的學生
艾蜜莉：行銷系的學生

情境對話 *Dialogue*

Ruth: I am glad that we are at the same group, Emily. I think we will make a great team.

露絲：很高興和妳同一組，艾蜜莉。我想我們會合作無間的。

Emily: You bet. First of all, we need to make a plan.

艾蜜莉：一點也沒錯；首先，我們需要制定個計劃。

Ruth: <u>What do you think if</u> we play advertisement on TV, Internet and print media?

露絲：妳覺得我們在電視、網路、平面媒體上刊登廣告怎麼樣？

Emily: TV commercials will cost a lot. Maybe we focus on social media because it fits most people's viewing habits and lifestyles nowadays.

艾蜜莉：電視預算很高。也許鎖定社交網路比較符合大多數人的收視習慣與生活習慣。

Ruth: Indeed. Moreover, the price of the handbag isn't very high. And the middle class <u>relies more</u> on social media.

露絲：嗯，而且手提包價格不是很貴。中產階級也更依賴社交網站。

Emily: You are right. We can evaluate the effectiveness of advertising after three weeks, and if it doesn't work out, we can change to other media.

艾蜜莉：妳說對了。我們也可以在三週後評估廣告成效，如果不如預期，可以改投其他媒體。

Ruth: For example, fashion magazines or newspapers.

露絲：例如，時尚雜誌或者報紙。

Emily: You are right again.

艾蜜莉：妳又說對了。

短句補給 Useful Phrases

✓ I think will will make a great team. 我想我們會合作無間的
✓ rely more on... 更加依賴…
✓ What do you think if...? 如果是…，你覺得如何？

1 行銷

2 廣告

3 媒體採購

4 公關公司

5 網路行銷

6 企業社會形象

Some of journalists are my friends. But sometimes they still write the things I told them not to write. If I keep a distance with them, then our relationship will have a little tension. I don't like the feeling to beg them write some articles for our new products.

有些記者我當他們是朋友。但是他們偶而還是會寫出一些我要他們不要寫的內容。如果我和他們保持距離，我們之間的關係就會有些緊繃。我真的很不喜歡拜託記者幫忙寫些稿子，來介紹我們的新品。

Dialogue 1　主題對話 25

Sometimes They Write the Things I Told Them Not to Write.
有時候，他們會寫些我不要他們寫的。

 情境說明 *Situation*

The public relations supervisor is discussing the media relations plan with marketing manager. The media relations budget is very limited this year. They need to come to an agreement on budget spending.

公關主任正在和行銷經理討論媒體關係的計劃，今年度的媒體關係預算很有限，因此他們得協調一下預算花費與分配。

情境對話 *Dialogue*

Marketing Manager: Could you please explain a bit regarding the media relations plan?

行銷經理：你可以解釋一下關於媒體關係的計劃嗎？

PR Supervisor: Sure. On the calendar, this year we are planning to launch 5 new products in Q2 and Q3. Therefore, the larger amount in Q2 and Q3 is for the press conferences of launches. We will come back to that later.

公關主任：當然。在行事曆上，今年度在第二季與第三季我們有五項新產品將要上市，因此，比較多的預算金額是規劃在舉辦這些新品的記者會，我們可以稍後再回頭討論這部分。

139

Marketing Manager: **Agree.**

行銷經理：同意。

PR Supervisor: **The Q1 is the CNY season. Usually we would prepare the CNY gift packs for chief editors or news channel managers. Last year, each gift pack costs us nearly $3,000. This year, I slightly reduced the price range. So the total budget could be decreased. Plus, we print the company CNY greeting card in the past years. Since we have printed the company Christmas card a few months ago, I suggest we could skip printing the CNY card.**

公關主任：每年的第一季是農曆新年的季節。往年這個時候，我們都會準備新年禮盒給主編們或新聞台的經理們，去年的經驗，每份禮盒大約採購費用為三千元，今年，我稍微減低了採購的額度，因此整體的預算花費將會降低。此外，以往我們會印製農曆新年賀卡，不過其實幾個月前，我們才印製了聖誕節賀卡，因此我建議可以省略印製農曆新年賀卡。

Marketing Manager: **I understand. Many other companies don't print the CNY greeting card in fact. They buy the existing greeting cards from the bookstores and stamp on the company logo.**

行銷經理：我了解，事實上，很多其他的公司都不會特別印製農曆新年賀卡，他們都會買書店裡現成的賀卡，然後印上公司的標示識別。

PR Supervisor: **I have seen that, too. But it's not sophisticated. I would use 10,000 NTD to hire a digital design house to design an e-Card. It's more efficiently and not costly at all.**

公關主任：我也看過。不過那看起來不是很精緻，我預計使用一萬元的預算，找一間數為設計公司，來製作一張電子賀卡。費用不貴又相當有效。

Marketing Manager: That's even better.

行銷經理：這樣更好。

PR Supervisor: Let's move on to the next part. We also send the birthday cakes to all chief editors and new channel manager of majority media on regular basis in the past years. But basing on their feedback, they don't seem to like the idea of sending a cake very much. As sometimes if they were on business trip, or out of office for certain reasons, no one would notice and open up the cakes. The cakes would just rotten. It's not a pleasant feeling at all to discover a rotten birthday cake for them.

公關主任：我們繼續看下一部份。往年，我們也會定期寄送生日蛋糕給主要媒體的主編與新聞部主管。但是根據他們的反應，他們似乎不太喜歡寄送生日蛋糕的這個點子。因為有些時候，當他們出差去，或是因為其他原因不在辦公室內，蛋糕會因為沒人發現或打開它而就這樣腐壞了，他們表示，事後看到自己的生日蛋糕發霉、發臭的感覺不是挺好。

Marketing Manager: If then, we could just cut off the birthday cake budget.

行銷經理：如果這樣，我們可不可以就直接移除生日蛋糕的預算？

PR Supervisor: No, I don't think so. They have been treating this way for years. If we suddenly cut off the cake budget, they would not know it was because of avoiding the rotten cake case. They would instead think we don't respect them as a media priority anymore.

公關主任：不妥，我不這樣想。這些人已經享受這樣的服務多年了，如果我們突然移除這筆預算，他們不會了解是因為我們想避免蛋糕腐壞的狀況，卻反而會認為，我們不再尊重他們，不再視他們為優先重要媒體。

1 行銷
2 廣告
3 媒體採購
4 公關公司
5 網路行銷
6 企業社會形象

Marketing Manager: So what would you suggest to do?

行銷經理：那麼你的建議是？

PR Supervisor: The cost of a cake is around 800 NTD, however, 800 NTD can't not really get any fine gift to surprise them. I would just send them a 1,000 NTD amount coupon to them. Since we buy every 100 coupons from department stores could get 20% discount.

公關主任：每個蛋糕的預算大約為新台幣八百元，不過以這樣的金額，很難挑到精美的禮物讓記者們驚豔，不如改寄面額一千元的禮券給他們。因為我們每買一百張百貨公司禮券，就可以打八折。

Marketing Manager: Perfect! Let's do that.

行銷經理：太好了！就這麼做。

PR Supervisor: In Q4, we used to arrange the media trip. The purpose is to entertain those very key media tycoons through touring our factories and head office. But the business class air tickets are getting more and more expensive due to the fuel price increasing. I think we could wipe the slate clean and stop the media tour.

公關主任：在第四季，我們以前都會安排媒體旅遊。這個目的是透過參觀工廠或總公司等旅遊來招待媒體大亨們，但是因為油價上漲，商務艙的機票價格也水漲船高，我想就此一掃這個習慣，停辦媒體旅遊。

Marketing Manager: How about what you mentioned earlier, they might think we don't respect them anymore?

行銷經理：不過你之前提到，他們也許會認為我們不再尊重他們？

PR Supervisor: The guests on media tour

公關主任：媒體旅遊的名單

list are only ten. Those are the VVIPs in the media industry. I will pay a visit to all of them in person to explain our situation.

Marketing Manager: We still need to engage the media in Q4 even we don't have new product launch.

PR Supervisor: That's correct. We could conduct a media gathering before the New Year. The general manager should join to show the sincerity given the fact that we lessen the overall treatment a bit. Also it's a great chance to socialize with journalists.

Marketing Manager: It's another way to entertain them.

PR Supervisor: Last but not least, always make the journalists feel they own us a favor. So the media would be friendlier to us.

上只有十位貴賓。他們是媒體圈非常非常重要的人士，我會親自一一拜訪，說明解釋我們的狀況。

行銷經理：在第四季，我們仍然需要與媒體互動、保持關係，即使沒有任何新品上市。

公關主任：沒錯。我們可以在跨年之前辦一場媒體餐敘，可以請總經理參加表現誠意，畢竟我們減少了一些媒體的招待，也是個機會與媒體記者交流、培養關係。

行銷經理：這也是另一種招待他們的方法。

公關主任：最後一點，但是也是很重要的一點，隨時讓記者們覺得他們欠我們一個人情，因此媒體也會對我們更友善些。

ABC 有料字彙 Vocabulary

- **chief** (*a.*) [tʃif] 主要的，重要的
  The **chief** aim of this season is to raise visibility.
  這一季最主要的目標是提高能見度。

- **slightly** (*adv.*) [`slaɪtlɪ] 稍微地
  He should be **slightly** tougher in that speech.
  那場演講他應該稍微地再強硬一點。

- **sophisticated** (*a.*) [sə`fɪstɪˌketɪd] 精緻的，精密的
  The product is known for its **sophisticated** design.
  這產品以精緻的設計聞名。

- **skip** (*v.*) [skɪp] 跳過，省略
  Let's **skip** this subject!
  讓我們跳過這個主題吧！

- **rotten** (*a.*) [`ratn] 腐敗的，發臭的
  The room is filled with the smell of **rotten** rats.
  那房間充滿了發臭老鼠的味道。

- **instead** (*adv.*) [ɪn`stɛd] 反而，替代地
  We use paper for gift wrapping **instead** of plastic this time.
  這次我們用紙代替塑膠做來為包裝材料。

- **tycoon** (*n.*) [taɪ`kun] 大亨，巨頭
  A **tycoon** is a very successful person in that business.
  所謂巨頭或大亨，就是在那領域中非常成功的人士。

- **slate** (*n.*) [slet] 石板，名單
  The company start a new business again with a clean **slate**.
  這家公司再一次拋開過去，開始全新事業。

- **gathering** (*n.*) [ˋgæðərɪŋ] 聚會，集會
  We will have weekly **gatherings** for at least three months.
  我們會有至少為期三個月的每週聚會。

- **socialize** (*v.*) [ˋsoʃəˌlaɪz] 社交，交際
  More than 30% of people **socialize** more online than they do face to face.
  有超過百分之三十的人透過網路社交比實際面對面的機會要更多。

有料句型 *Sentence Pattern*

句型 1 ↘

wipe the slate clean　重新來過；一筆勾銷

We could **wipe the slate clean**.
我們可以重新來過。

I don't own him a cent. I've **wipe the slate clean**.
我不欠他任何一毛錢，我的舊債已經一筆勾銷。

Let's just **wipe the slate clean** for the New Year!
新的一年，讓我們重新來過吧！

句型 2 ↘

Given the fact that A, B.　在 A 的情況下，有 B 的結果。

Given the fact that we lessen the overall treatment a bit, the general manager should join to show the sincerity.
在我們減少了一些媒體的招待的情況下，總經理可以來參與以表現誠意。

Given the fact that this huge number of replications, mistakes are

bound to happen.
因為複製的數量非常龐大，出錯在所難免。

I gave her a promotion **given the fact that** she's a good employee.
由於她是一個很棒的員工，我升了她的職。

Given the fact that the Chinese banks have similar business operation, the difference in practical process is the main competitive factor.
在所有銀行都提供類似的服務情況下，能夠在流程中展現區別，便是最主要的競爭重點。

1 行銷

2 廣告

3 媒體採購

4 公關公司

5 網路行銷

6 企業社會形象

Expert Tips
知識補給

The media relation seems very simple and yet it's also very complicated. You have to remain a friendly interaction with the journalists, see them as good partners and work together when heated situation. However, most importantly, never forget they are journalists.

媒體關係看起來很簡單，但是其實也相對地很複雜。你必須和媒體記者維持友善的互動、將他們當成是夥伴，也得在緊急的狀況下與他們共同工作。然而，最重要的是，永遠不要忘記他們是媒體記者。

Dialogue 2　延伸對話

Try to Improve The Relationship With Medias.
試著增進媒體關係。

 情境說明 *Situation*

Pearce and Zoe are two employees of a PR company, and they are planning this year's Media Day for the client.

皮爾斯與柔伊是公關公司的兩位專員，他們正在替客戶規劃今年的媒體日。

♀♂角色介紹 *Characters*

Zoe: Account Executive
Pearce: Account Executive

柔伊：專案執行
皮爾斯：專案執行

💬 **情境對話** *Dialogue*

Zoe: It's an annual Media Day again, I think we really have to come out with a unique event in order to improve the relationship with medias.

柔伊：又到了一年一度的媒體日，我想我們今年真的需要特別的活動，增進和媒體的關係。

Pearce: Indeed! Especially we had a problem at previous PR event, so, we need more positive reports to balance the

皮爾斯：真的！尤其是之前公關活動出了點問題，需要多點正面報導來平衡上個月

negative reports from last month.

的負面消息。

Zoe: What's in your mind?

柔伊：你有任何想法嗎？

Pearce: Since the client's product is sneakers, I am thinking maybe we can host an indoor sport game?

皮爾斯：竟然客戶的商品是球鞋，不如舉行一場室內競技怎麼樣？

Zoe: You mean, the reporters can wear our sneakers, and the prize goes to whoever wins the game in the end.

柔伊：你是說，記者們可以穿上客戶的球鞋，贏的人可以獲得獎品？

Pearce: We can even invite brand spokesman to join the competition!

皮爾斯：甚至可以邀請品牌代言人也來比賽！

Zoe: What a great idea! How did you come out with this?

柔伊：這真是個好點子！你是怎麼想出來的？

Pearce: Well, I am a natural born sports player.

皮爾斯：沒辦法，我可是天生運動好手呢！

短句補給 Useful Phrases

✓ What's in your mind? 你有任何想法嗎？
✓ What a great idea! 真是個好點子！
✓ I am a natural born sports player. 我可是天生的運動好手!

具有「企業造型師」功能的公關人員或公關公司，除了為企業打造形象之外，也負責情報蒐集，處理突發事件或緊急危機處理等，與其他部門一樣，在企業中有著不可或缺的地位。

4.

公關公司

PR Agency

公關公司管理
Key Visual Shooting

I would share most information, strategies and guidelines I have to the PR agency whose is handling our project. Because they are maybe the PR experts, but without understanding my company culture, project background, communication history and clear budget plan, I don't think they could ever meet my expectation.

我會分享所有的訊息、策略與規章給正在處理我們案子的公關公司，因為即便他們可能是公關專家，但是如果沒有清楚了解公司文化、案子的背景、前後溝通的過程，及清楚的預算計劃，我不認為他們可能達到我的期望。

1 行銷
2 廣告
3 媒體採購
4 公關公司
5 網路行銷
6 企業社會形象

Dialogue 1　主題對話

I Believe This Project Is in Good Hands.
我相信，這案子大家都會處理妥當的。

 情境說明 *Situation*

Previously, the former PR executive Danny was the contact person with the PR agency for the upcoming launch event. Unfortunately, Danny started to complain about the agency from time to time, a few months later, he resigned the job. The agency is updating the status to the PR supervisor.

先前，公關專員丹尼是負責與公關公司聯絡的人，主要是為了即將到來的上市活動。可惜的是，丹尼開始時不時地抱怨這間公關公司，幾個月後，他辭去了工作。公關公司目前正與公關主任進行著案子進度的簡報。

情境對話 *Dialogue*

PR supervisor: We only have one month left to prepare the event. But I noticed that a few important things like event venue, décor theme and reveal scene design are not confirmed yet. Please update the status so we can catch up on plan ASAP.

公關主任：我們只剩下一個月的活動準備時間，但是我注意到有幾個很重要的部分，尚未確認，例如活動場地、設計裝飾主題，產品揭幕儀式等等，請儘速説明進度，我們才能加緊腳步趕上進度。

Agency: The venue we originally preferred

公關公司：那個我們本來喜

and agreed has been booked until the end of next month. Therefore, we booked another similar venue and updated to Danny three weeks ago. But Danny didn't like to change venue and he wanted us keeping negotiating the possibility of using the original venue.

歡且都同意的場地,已經被訂到下個月底,因此我們訂了另一個類似的場地,我們在三週前告訴丹尼這個消息,但是他不喜歡變更場地,希望我們繼續與原場地洽談,看看有沒有機會仍然可以訂到位子。

PR supervisor: If the venue is not confirmed, it's not possible to print on invitation also measure the décor boards. Given the circumstances, I agree to use the substitute venue.

公關主任:如果場地一直沒有被確認,是不可能完成邀請函的印刷,以及丈量製作場地裝飾背板等。依照現在的情況看來,我同意使用替代的場地。

Agency: Great! As the décor theme, we proposed "old fashion black and white" or "back to 80's" basing on the brand was once super popular in 80's. Another theme was "pinky lover" since the Valentine's day is approaching.

公關公司:太好了!關於場地設計裝飾,因為這個品牌曾經在八〇年代非常受歡迎,因此我們提案了『復古黑與白』、『重回八〇』兩種風格,另一提案風格是『粉紅情人』,主要是因為情人節快到了的應景主題。

PR supervisor: None of them are acceptable. Basically, our strategy is to create the high tech impression and don't

公關主任:上述這些都不可行,基本上,我們的策略是創造一個高科技的形象,且

want to mention the past glory. Female consumers are not our major TAs. I would share with you the brand strategy and vision after this meeting.

不要重提舊日光彩。女性消費者也不是我們的產品對象。我會在會後提供品牌策略與願景給你們。

Agency: High tech impression. I get it now.

公關公司：高科技形象，我現在知道了。

PR supervisor: Not just the décor theme, I am thinking that the product reveal design could also go with this direction. Use high tech tools to reveal the product. But please avoid any perplexity design as a result of time and budget limitation.

公關主任：不止是場地設計裝飾，包括產品揭幕儀式也是要走同樣的路線，可以使用高科技工具來呈現，但是請避免複雜難懂的設計，因為時間與經費有限。

Agency: Frankly speaking, that direction came across our minds. We thought about metal sliver and wavy pattern, icy but diversified.

公關公司：坦白説，我們其實想過這個方向，我們想用銀色金屬風格，配上一些水波圖案，冷調卻變化多端。

PR supervisor: Sounds cool, please propose it tomorrow. What is the status of special guest inviting which we have been talking about last month?

公關主任：聽起來很不錯，請明天正式提案吧。另外活動嘉賓的邀請，我們從上個月就一直說到現在，情況如何？

Agency: It's under control.

公關公司：在掌握之中。

1 行銷

2 廣告

3 媒體採購

4 公關公司

5 網路行銷

6 企業社會形象

PR supervisor: What do you mean under control? Did you sign the contract with that celebrity?

公關主任：在掌握中的意思是？已經和藝人簽了合約了嗎？

Agency: Not yet, but we have spoke with the agent and also she orally agreed to participant.

公關公司：還沒有，但是我們已經與經紀人通過電話，她口頭同意來參加。

PR supervisor: Then I would like to have it in written. That makes the whole thing more secure.

公關主任：那麼我希望儘速付諸於文字，讓整件事情更穩當。

Agency: Right. We will call the agent tomorrow.

公關公司：好的，我們明天打電話給經紀人。

PR supervisor: I believe this project is in good hands. To help me more involved, every Monday morning at 10, I would like to call an update meeting. So we can all have a face-to-face talk and solve the issues on time.

公關主任：我相信這個案子大家都會處理得妥當，為了幫助我多一些進入狀況，每個星期一上午十點，我希望有個進度會議，我們可以因此面對面解決遇到的問題。

1 行銷

2 廣告

3 媒體採購

4 公關公司

5 網路行銷

6 企業社會形象

ABC 有料字彙 Vocabulary

- **substitute** (*a.*) [ˋsʌbstəˌtjut] 代替的，替補的
  Jack is taking a sick leave today and that tall man is to **substitute** him.
  Jack 今天請病假，那位高個子的先生會代替他。

- **reveal** (*v.*) [rɪˋvil] 展現，揭示
  The color you choose **reveals** your personality.
  你選的顏色透露了你的性格。

- **scene** (*n.*) [sin] 場面，景象
  I can't get rid of the **scene** when the two lovers died in that play.
  我無法抹去劇中那兩個情人死去時的場景。

- **venue** (*n.*) [ˋvɛnju] 場地，地點
  Please do not change the **venue** at will.
  請不要隨便更改地點。

- **circumstance** (*n.*) [ˋsɝkəmˌstæns] 環境，情況
  I want her to be there under no **circumstances**.
  無論任何情況下，我要她到場。

- **approach** (*v.*) [əˋprotʃ] 接近，即將達到
  The host suddenly **approached** the audience.
  主持人突然接近那位觀眾。

- **perplexity** (*n.*) [pɚˋplɛksɪtɪ] 困惑，糾結
  There is a look of **perplexity** and surprise on her face.
  她臉上有困惑和驚喜的表情。

- **diversified** (*a.*) [daɪˋvɝsəˌfaɪ] 多樣化的
  This company offers **diversified** products to meet customers' needs.
  這家公司提供多樣化的產品滿足顧客需求。

· **pattern** (*n.*) [`pætɚn] 花樣，圖案

They just love these grid **patterns**.

他們就愛這格子圖案。

有料句型 Sentence Pattern

句型 1 ↘

as a result of... 由於⋯

Please avoid any perplexity design **as a result of** time and budget limitation.

由於時間與經費有限，請避免複雜難懂的設計。

The plan foundered **as a result of** lack of finance.

這個計劃由於缺乏資金而失敗。

She died **as a result of** her injuries.

她由於受傷而死。

句型 2 ↘

in good hands （被）妥當處理；（得到）良好照顧

I believe this project is **in good hands**.

我相信這案子會備妥善處理的。

This garage is excellent; your car will be **in good hands**.

這個車廠棒極了，你的車將會被處理得妥當。

If you go to Dr. Wu, you are **in good hands**.

如果你給吳醫生主治，你就找對了人。

1 行銷

2 廣告

3 媒體採購

4 公關公司

5 網路行銷

6 企業社會形象

Expert Tips
知識補給

The key of PR agency management is treating them as a new partner/comer of your company. Trust them, love them but still check the facts. Plus, you should insist on the regular meetings and updates.

公關公司管理的重點在於，對待他們如同一公司的新進夥伴／同事。相信他們，關愛他們，但是仍然不要忘了時常檢視事實狀況。此外，要維持召開定期進度報告與會議。

Dialogue 2　延伸對話 　　　　　　　　　　　　◎28

Set the PR Goals 設定公關目標

 情境說明 *Situation*

Betty came to Robert's office, and they are going to set the PR goals for the publicity campaign of Japanese celebrity in Taiwan .

貝蒂來到了羅伯的辦公室，他們將要針對日本藝人來台的宣傳活動，設定公關任務目標。

♀♂**角色介紹** *Characters*

Robert: PR Manager
Betty: Project Manager of Y PR Company

羅伯：公關經理
貝蒂：Y 公關公司的專案經理

💬 **情境對話** *Dialogue*

Robert: Hello, Betty. It's nice to have you in our office.

羅伯：你好，貝蒂。很高興妳來到我們公司。

Betty: Thank you. I look forward to today's meeting since last week.

貝蒂：謝謝你。我從上週就開始期待今天的見面。

Robert: Then, we'd better start it now. I am thinking this event should reach more

羅伯：那麼我們現在就開始吧。我希望這次活動可以獲

than thirty media exposures.

得 30 篇的報導曝光。

Betty: Including print media, Internet, TV and weekly magazines?

貝蒂：包括平面媒體、網路、電視和週刊？

Robert: Yes. <u>Is there a problem?</u>

羅伯：是的。有問題嗎？

Betty: Not at all. I guess it might be over this number.

貝蒂：沒有。我想可能會超過這個數字。

Robert: That would be great. Moreover, I hope there will be more than fifty medias attend autograph signing.

羅伯：那就太好了。另外，我希望有 50 家以上的媒體出席簽名會。

Betty: It could be a little bit too many. Let's set a range from twenty-five to thirty-five?

貝蒂：這數字有點多了。不如我們訂個範圍吧，25 到 35 家媒體呢？

Robert: All right. But if you couldn't reach it, I want to see the analyzing report.

羅伯：好吧。但是如果沒有達到這個數字，我要看到檢討報告。

短句補給 Useful Phrases

✓ It's nice to have you in our office. 很高興你來到我們公司。
✓ We'd better start it now.　我們最好現在就開始。
✓ Is there a problem?　有問題嗎？

上市記者會安排
Press Conference

We are about to launch a series of skin care products. Although we started to prepare from long ago, many issues still come along. My learning is, stay calm while shooting the issues.

　　我們即將要上市一個皮膚保養產品的系列。雖然我們從很早之前就開始計劃，但是太多的狀況與問題還是一一發生，我學到的是，面對與解決問題時，要沉著穩定。

1 行銷

2 廣告

3 媒體採購

4 公關公司

5 網路行銷

6 企業社會形象

Dialogue 1　主題對話 29

We Are Going to Wrap the Whole Thing in Mystery.
我們要把這整個弄得很神秘。

 情境說明 *Situation*

Taiwan is the first market to launch this product series. The product is made in France. As the press conference date is approaching, we still have not received the product testers, product visuals, package designs and product samples.

台灣是全球第一個上市這個系列產品的市場，而產品是在法國製造。隨著記者會的日子一天天逼近，我們到現在都沒有收到試用品、產品照、包裝設計圖，以及樣品。

情境對話 *Dialogue*

Marketing Manager: Have you heard from Paris office about the visuals and package design files?

行銷經理：關於照片與包裝設計檔，請問你有得到巴黎辦公室的消息了嗎？

Marketing Specialist: Not really. They only sent one product shot with very low resolution and it cannot be used the stage backdrop printing. Besides, we are launching the whole series, 6 items. Only one picture is really helping.

行銷專員：不完全有。他們只寄了一張產品照過來，解析度還相當低，因此不能輸出印刷成舞台背板。此外，我們要上市的一系列共有六支產品，現在只有其中一支的產品照，實在幫不了大忙。

Marketing Manager: Do we have any sample here? If we do, then we can send it to the studio to shot the visuals locally.

行銷經理：我們的產品樣品到貨了嗎？如果已經到了，我們可以送到附近的攝影棚去拍產品照。

Marketing Specialist: No, the samples and testers are not here yet. They said the shipment would be arrived one day after the press conference.

行銷專員：沒有。產品完整包裝的樣品和試用品都沒有到，他們説船期剛好落在記者會後的第二天。

Marketing Manager: I recognized the color of package is purple, check its Pantone color number and use the color to décor the whole venue. Meanwhile, please send the low-resolution file to the photo house and see if they can do any way to enlarge the resolution.

行銷經理：我記得包裝的顏色是紫色，查一下這個顏色的「彩通 Pantone」號碼，整個記者會場就用這個色調來佈置。同時，請將那個低解析度的檔案交給攝影公司，看看他們有沒有任何辦法可以提高解析度。

Marketing Specialist: Even if we have one high-resolution visual, but we don't have testers in the press conference for the media to try. Not to mention there would be no free sample for them to take home with the press kit.

行銷專員：就算我們有了一張高解析度的照片，但是我們沒有任何試用品，提供給媒體客人在記者會上試用，更不要説在記者資料袋裡，也沒有任何樣品可以放。

Marketing Manager: I know. <u>We have to wrap the whole thing in mystery</u>. Make the media feel curious and exciting about it. Hope them would buy in.

行銷經理：我知道，所以我們要包裝整個活動在一個神秘氣氛裡，讓媒體期待且好奇我們的新品。希望記者們會買單。

Marketing Specialist: What product could we put it into the press kit?

行銷專員：我們可以放什麼產品到記者資料袋裡呢？

Marketing Manager: I think we imported 300 sample bottles of another series a few months ago. But afterward we decided not to launch it. We could use those samples and tell the media "a special Christmas gift that you cannot purchase in Taiwan yet."

行銷經理：我想幾個月前，曾經進了一批另一個系列的樣品，約三百瓶，不過後來我們決定不上是這一款。我們可以將這些樣品放入資料袋，告訴媒體「一個在台灣還買不到的特別聖誕節禮物」。

Marketing Specialist: What was the reason that we decided not to launch that series?

行銷專員：當時是什麼原因，讓我們決定不上市這一系列？

Marketing Manager: It was because of Taiwan regulations. The ingredients need more time to get the approval.

行銷經理：那是因為台灣法規，這一系列的產品的成分需要較多的時間取得許可證。

Marketing Specialist: The good news is both series are sharing the same sweet orange fragrance. The press conference date happens to be Christmas. I think the media would not mind just try the smell only. Plus, they receive some very special gifts.

行銷專員：好消息是，兩個系列所使用的香精味道，都是甜橙。由於記者會當天剛好是聖誕節，我想媒體們應該不會介意只試用到香味，加上，他們還會收到一份特別的禮物。

Marketing Manager: The thing I am worried about is all the products could be

行銷經理：我擔心的是，所有的產品是否能夠到貨，在

ready to sell in 500 counters in department stores on Jan 1st?

一月一日當天全部五百家百貨公司櫃檯都能夠開賣。

Marketing Specialist: I checked with Product Supply Dept. They are quite confident.

行銷專員：我與產品通路部門查詢過了，他們頗有信心。

Marketing Manager: Right, let's talk about the product display in the press conference venue. What is your contingency plan?

行銷經理：好。我們談談在記者會當天，會場的產品展示該怎麼處理？你有什麼應變計劃？

Marketing Specialist: I will use the one and only low-resolution visual to do it. Create a plastic white Christmas tree with a height of 200cm, hanging 200 transparent balls on the tree. Every sealed ball has one mini product mock-up inside.

行銷專員：我會用那張唯一的低解析度照片來處理。設計一個高約二公尺的白色塑膠聖誕樹，上面掛了約二百個透明的球，每個密封的球裡面，都會有一個迷你的產品樣。

Marketing Manager: The media cannot touch it to try on, but they can only see product package all over the place.

行銷經理：所以媒體們碰不到，也不能打開試用，卻整個會場都是產品的視覺。

Marketing Specialist: Yes, that is the idea.

行銷專員：是的，就是這個意思。

1 行銷

2 廣告

3 媒體採購

4 公關公司

5 網路行銷

6 企業社會形象

ABC 有料字彙 Vocabulary

- **tester** (*n.*) [ˋtɛstə] 試用品

  These perfume **testers** are perfect giveaway items for office ladies.

  這些香水試聞瓶是給粉領族最佳的贈品品項。

- **resolution** (*n.*) [ˏrɛzəˋluʃən] 解析度

  We need higher image **resolution** for the outdoor signboard.

  我們需要更高解析度的圖來製作戶外看板。

- **backdrop** (*n.*) [ˋbækˏdrɑp] 背景幕，背板

  We use a red cardboard as a **backdrop** to set the Christmas mood.

  我們用紅色紙板當做背景板安排出聖誕節的心情。

- **mystery** (*n.*) [ˋmɪstərɪ] 神秘的事物，秘密

  She is always a **mystery** to him.

  她對他而言永遠是個謎。

- **fragrance** (*n.*) [ˋfregrəns] 香精，香料

  The sweet **fragrance** is coming from that room.

  甜甜的香味從那房間傳出來。

- **contingency** (*n.*) [kənˋtɪndʒənsɪ] 偶然事件，意外事件

  Always have a backup plan and be prepared for any **contingency**.

- **transparent** (*a.*) [trænsˋpɛrənt] 透明的，可看透的

  We are going to put the magician in a **transparent** plastic container.

  我們要把魔術師放進一個透明的塑膠箱子裡。

🐥🐥**有料句型** *Sentence Pattern*

句型 1↘

A be wrapped in B　A（被）包覆在 B 裡面

They **are wrapped in** the night of ignorance.
他們完全蒙昧無知。

I seemed to **be wrapped in** a kind of mist.
我似乎被一種迷霧籠罩住了。

He **is all wrapped up in** his scientific studies.
他完全埋首於他的科學研究中。

句型 2↘

happen to　剛好是；恰巧是

The press conference date **happens to** be Christmas.
記者會的日子恰巧是聖誕節。

It **happened to** be a Sunday.
那天剛好是星期天。

Both of them **happened to** be there.
他們倆剛好都在那。

1 行銷

2 廣告

3 媒體採購

4 公關公司

5 網路行銷

6 企業社會形象

Expert Tips
知識補給

Holding a press conference needs a few actions: define messages, select venue/date/time/participants, invite media, develop press kit and product display etc. However, the reality is harsh sometimes. Therefore, preparing yourself to deal with urgent matters is needed.

　　舉辦一場記者會需要一些事前工作，確認溝通的訊息、選好場地、日期、時間、參加者、邀請媒體、準備記者資料袋、產品會場展示等等。不過，現實有時候卻很嚴酷，所以讓自己做好應變緊急狀況的準備，也是必要的。

Dialogue 2　延伸對話　🔊30

Wish You Can Make It in Time. 希望你們可以及時趕上。

☕ 情境說明 *Situation*

Jennifer and Ted are confirming some details of the press conference of a new product.

珍妮佛和泰德正在確認一款新產品上市發表會的細節。

♀♂ 角色介紹 *Characters*

Jennifer: PR Account Executive of Z Company
Ted: PR Assistant Manager of S Hotel

珍妮佛：Z 公司的公關專員
泰德：S 飯店公關部副理

💬 情境對話 *Dialogue*

Jennifer: I cannot believe the event is coming on this Friday.

珍妮佛：真不敢相信活動就在這週五了。

Ted: Yap, I feel the same way. Let's start to check the details, because I am going to the <u>take a personal leave</u> one hour later.

泰德：有同感。我們現在開始確認細節吧，一小時候我請事假呢。

Jennifer: Sure. Now I only need to confirm news release and talking points of General

珍妮佛：好的。我只剩下新聞稿和總經理的演講大綱還

170

Manager's speech.

待確認。

Ted: <u>Wish you can make it on time.</u> By the way, you haven't told me yet which kind of snacks you need on that day.

泰德：希望你們可以及時趕上。對了，妳還沒有告訴我當天需要哪款點心？

Jennifer: I remember that I sent you an email last Thursday.

珍妮佛：我記得上週四寄電子郵件給你了。

Ted: Then you said that your Boss wants to change them.

泰德：後來妳又說妳的主管想要換。

Jennifer: Holly shit! <u>I totally forgot it.</u> I am calling back to the office right now.

珍妮佛：真糟糕！我完全忘了此事。我馬上打電話回公司詢問。

Ted: Then please also ask why they haven't paid the deposit for booking the revenue.

泰德：那麼也請問問為什麼場地的訂金還沒有付吧。

短句補給 Useful Phrases

✓ Take a personal leave.　請事假。
✓ Wish you can make it on time.　希望你(們)可以及時趕上。
✓ I totally forgot it.　我完全忘記了。

4-3 展覽活動策劃
Road Show

There are a million things that need to be prepared before a road show, from venue design and showgirl selection to product display, giveaway item production, product specification sheets and so on. Usually you have only 2 months to prepare. And it's still a challenge even when you have plenty of lead time.

一場展覽活動的事前準備工作很繁重。從場地設計、展示人員選擇、產品陳列、贈品製作、與產品規格表確認等,通常的籌備期間會從兩個月前開始,但是即便時間充足,仍然會是一個挑戰。

1 行銷

2 廣告

3 媒體採購

4 公關公司

5 網路行銷

6 企業社會形象

Dialogue 1　主題對話 31

Make Sure It's Supported with Proper Merchandising and Staffing.
要確定有適當的貨品推銷規劃和人力配置。

 情境說明 *Situation*

Planning and preparation for the roadshow is approaching the final phase. Now the marketing manager and sales manager are having a final discussion before announcing all the details to the team in a pre-meeting.

目前展覽活動的規劃已經接近最後階段，行銷經理與業務經理正在開會討論，決定在行前會議時公佈給團隊的內容。

情境對話 *Dialogue*

Marketing Manager: I would like to update you on the status of the road show, and we'll also need some support from your team.

行銷經理：我這裡先和你說明一下目前進度，以及我們會需要你的團隊協助的地方。

Sales Manager: Of course. We are all very excited about the road show.

業務經理：當然，我們都很期待這場展覽。

Marketing Manager: A pre-meeting will be conducted one week before the road show. Our booth is number 120 and located at the east end of the exhibition

行銷經理：展覽正式開始的前一週，我們將安排一場行前會議。我們的攤位號碼是 120 號，位於展覽廳的東

173

hall.

Sales Manager: How big is our booth? Is it close to the nearest entry door?

Marketing Manager: No. It's a pity, but our booth is not very close to the gate. They drew lots to decide the location. The size is around 2,000 feet. Since you brought up booth size, I would like to know: How many cars do you want to display? Could you provide me a list of the models and colors? I would like to display our newest model, which will be launched in December.

Sales Manager: I am thinking about displaying 12 cars. That newest model should definitely attract attention. But you'll have to check the shipment and delivery date. I hope it can arrive on time!

Marketing Manager: You're right. I also have to check with the designer about whether we can display 12 cars, as we also need to consider the size of the employee rest area and guest reception area.

邊位置。

業務經理：攤位有多大？是否接近出口？

行銷經理：我們的位置不是很接近出口，但是這是投票出來的結果。大小約為 2,000 尺，不過既然你提到了攤位大小，我也剛好想問你，你預計想展示幾部車呢？你可以給我一張清單，你想展示的車款與顏色嗎？我想展示那部最新型號，在十二月即將上市的車款。

業務經理：我想展示 12 部車，那部最新型號的車款確實會引起目光焦點，但是你得確定一下船期與抵港出關日，希望能趕上！

行銷經理：你說的對，另外，我也得和設計師確定一下，展場的位置夠不夠放得下 12 部車，我們必須考慮到員工休息區與賓客接待區。

1 行銷

2 廣告

3 媒體採購

4 公關公司

5 網路行銷

6 企業社會形象

Sales Manager: Understood. I will select the eight most important cars to show, just in case we cannot show all 12. Just a reminder, please don't forget the Internet set up. Our guests like free Wi-Fi very much, so if we have it they will stay longer at our booth.

業務經理：那我先安排 8 部優先展示車的款式，提醒一下，別忘了網路的架設，賓客們都很喜歡免費網路的服務，他們便會在我們的攤位停留久一點。

Marketing Manager: Sure. According to the rules, the purchase of products is not allowed at the venue, so please have your sales team collect guest contact information to close the deal later, but do not show any purchase contracts during the road show. Also, please share the shift arrangement schedule with me next week.

行銷經理：當然。不過根據法規，在會場內是不可以有任何銷售行為，因此，請讓你的業務代表們，記得留下賓客的聯絡資訊，以便後續的接洽與確認訂單。請務必確認在展場內不會出現購買契約。另一方面，請下個星期提供給我業務代表們的值班表。

Sales Manager: I will.

業務經理：我會的。

Marketing Manager: When do you think would be a proper date to have the pre-meeting with the sales team?

行銷經理：你覺得哪一天安排行前會議，對業務部比較方便？

Sales Manager: Next Tuesday afternoon could be good timing, as all area sales managers will be in Taipei.

業務經理：下個星期二下午的時間很合適，因為剛好所有的區域業務經理都在臺北。

Marketing Manager: Great! At the pre-meeting, I will also explain the details of the showgirl performance schedule, gift item giveaway, employee pass distribution, and media visit dates.

行銷經理：那很好。我會一併與大家說明展示人員的排班時間表、小禮物的贈送、員工通行證與媒體訪問拍照日的細節。

Sales Manager: We should wear our regular company tie and nametag during the road show, right?

業務經理：我們都應該戴上公司領帶，並別上個人名牌。是嗎？

Marketing Manager: Correct.

行銷經理：正確。

1 行銷

2 廣告

3 媒體採購

4 公關公司

5 網路行銷

6 企業社會形象

ABC 有料字彙 Vocabulary

- **road show** (*n.*) 巡迴演出
  The **road show** includes a multimedia presentation and question-and-answer sessions.
  這場演出包括有多媒體展示以及問與答。

- **lead time** (*n.*) 前置準備時間
  I didn't have enough **lead time** to get all things done.
  我沒有足夠的前置時間把所有事情做好。

- **merchandising** (*n.*) [ˋmɝtʃənˌdaɪzɪŋ] 貨品的推銷規劃
  Merchandising involves the display and sales strategies.
  貨品的推銷規劃包含了陳列及銷售的策略。

- **staffing** (*n.*) [ˋstæfɪŋ] 人員配置
  Staffing and budget shortages are our major problems.
  我們的主要問題是人員和預算短缺。

- **attract** (*v.*) [əˋträkt] 吸引
  What **attracted** me most to the road show was the giant balloon.
  這演出最吸引我的地方是那顆巨大的汽球。

- **employee** (*n.*) [ˌɛmplɔɪˋi] 員工；僱員
  Employees are seeking greater meaning from their work.
  員工正從工作中找尋更大的意義。

- **reception** (*n.*) [rɪˋsɛpʃən] 接待
  They gave me a passionate **reception**.
  他們給了我一個熱情的接待。

- **shift** (*n.*) [ʃɪft] 輪班；輪班工作時間
  She works on night **shift**.
  她上晚班。

🐦🐦 有料句型 Sentence Pattern

句型 1 ↘

... is approaching the final phase. …（接近）到達最後階段了。

Planning and preparation for the road show **is approaching the final phase**.
演出的計劃和準備已經接近最後階段了。

The therapy **is approaching the final phase**.
治療到達最後階段。

The three-day event **is approaching the final phase**.
為期三天的活動已到達最後階段了。

句型 2 ↘

Just a reminder, ... （只是）提醒一下...

Just a reminder, please don't forget the Internet set up.
提醒一下，別忘了網路的設定。

Just a reminder, we should wear our nametags during the whole show.
提醒一下，我們應該要全程都帶著名牌。

Just a reminder, bring your name cards in case you need them.
提醒一下，名片帶著，以防萬一。

1 行銷

2 廣告

3 媒體採購

4 公關公司

5 網路行銷

6 企業社會形象

Expert Tips
知識補給

Road shows give retailers an opportunity to offer their customers unique products beyond their normal inventory selection, or provide them special promotional prices. The average duration of a road show can be from 4 to 18 days in multiple cities. If supported with proper merchandising and staffing, a road show allows a retailer to offer customers new and exciting merchandise, increase frequency of shopper visits, and a create a sense of urgency to buy the featured product before the road show ends.

展覽活動通常展示得不只庫存商品，尤其是特殊商品，這是銷售商吸引消費者注意的大好時機，也是提供消費者特別促銷價的時候。一場展覽活動的平均展期可以從四天到十八天，在多個城市進行，它需要適當的產品展示量，以及人力安排，銷售商利用令人驚豔的展場設計，引起消費者的新鮮感，增加買家蒞臨攤位的次數與頻率，在展覽活動結束前刺激買氣。

Dialogue 2　延伸對話 32

I Have a Bottleneck in This Project. 我遇到瓶頸了。

 情境說明 *Situation*

For upcoming art exhibition event, Cindy goes to meet her Manager, Hugh.

為了即將到來的藝術展覽活動，辛蒂去見她的主管，休。

♀♂**角色介紹** *Characters*

Cindy: Event Assistant
Hugh: Event Manager

辛蒂：活動專員
休：活動經理

 情境對話 *Dialogue*

Cindy: Hi, Boss. I think I have a bottleneck in this project.

辛蒂：嗨，老大。我想這個專案上我遇到瓶頸了。

Hugh: I am listening.

休：説來聽聽。

Cindy: It's about the art exhibition next month. We haven't confirmed the stage design yet.

辛蒂：就是下個月的藝術展覽活動，舞台設計還沒有確認。

Hugh: I think I will let you know this afternoon.

休：我想下午我就會讓妳知道結果了。

Cindy: That would be great. And there are some art works might not join us this time.

辛蒂：那太好了。還有，有幾個作品可能會缺席。

Hugh: Then perhaps we can use the space as a Gift Shop.

休：那就把空間規劃成禮品店吧。

Cindy: OK. I am also thinking maybe we can host few seminars, and inviting the art creators to have communications with art lovers.

辛蒂：好。另外，我也在想是不是能辦幾場座談會，請作家現身與愛好者交流。

Hugh: Great idea! Make sure that if we invite famous art creators, we have to charge for admission fee.

休：好點子！如果請到知名的作家，記得要收入場費。

短句補給 Useful Phrases

✓ I have a bottleneck in… 我在…上遇到瓶頸了。
✓ I am listening. 説來聽聽、洗耳恭聽。
✓ Charge admission fee. 收入場費。

1 行銷

2 廣告

3 媒體採購

4 公關公司

5 網路行銷

6 企業社會形象

4-4 新聞稿與聲明稿
News Release & Statement

An urgent meeting was just called. Almost all the media are producing very large pieces reporting on our product's nutritional content and its effect on health. I am really worried about what to do.

一場緊急的會議剛剛召開。今天幾乎所有的媒體,都用了很大的篇幅報導我們產品的營養成分與對健康的影響。我真的很擔心該怎麼辦。

1 行銷

2 廣告

3 媒體採購

4 公關公司

5 網路行銷

6 企業社會形象

Dialogue 1　主題對話

Timing Is Crucial. 時間點很重要。

情境說明 Situation

A competing brand made an allusion to the unhealthiness of our products two days ago. We are now having a contingency meeting to determine the next step.

兩天前，一個競爭對手的品牌用了隱喻的方式，形容了我們的產品是不健康的。我們現在正在召開一個緊急應變會議，討論下一步的因應對策。

情境對話 Dialogue

PR Manager: Allow me to debrief you on the situation. Two days ago our competitor attacked us by using a media advertorial saying our potato chips contain excessive olein. They said our product is too greasy and unhealthy. In addition to the advertorial, yesterday a news release was issued with a comparison of their products to ours. This morning, many journalists contacted me and tried to get our official feedback regarding this topic.

公關經理：讓我在這裡簡單說明一下狀況。我們的競爭品牌在前幾天用廣編稿的方式攻擊我們的產品含油量過高，並強調我們的產品太油膩且不健康，不止是登出廣編稿，昨天還發表了一篇新聞稿，內容關於兩家產品的比較。今天一早，陸續許多記者便開始聯絡我，希望得到我們品牌對於這些言論的看法。

R&D Manager: The fact is, their comparison is actually truthful. Our products do contain more oil than theirs. <u>We fry our products, while they bake theirs.</u> That makes a difference.

研發經理：事實上，他們所做的產品比較表上的內容，是實際的狀況。我們的產品的確含了比較多油，因為我們是用油炸方式處理，而他們是用烤的，這就有很大的差別。

Marketing Manager: We have to be very careful on this issue. Do you suggest we should issue a news release, too?

行銷經理：我們必須很小心地處理這個議題，你建議我們應該要發表一份新聞稿嗎？

PR Manager: A news release is more about sharing positive news, product information, and corporate news, and announcing and describing events, using an official but gentle tone and manner. <u>When a brand is facing a public issue, I would suggest issuing a brand statement or company statement.</u> The purpose of the statement is to clarify the brand or company position, and provide brand or company feedback and comments on a given heated issue.

公關經理：新聞稿通常是公佈一些較為正面的新聞內容，比如產品發表，企業消息，活動訊息或成果，用一種正式但又禮貌的敘述。當品牌面對到公眾問題時，我們建議應該要發表一份公司或品牌的聲明稿，一份聲明稿主要的目的是澄清說明公司或品牌對於發燒議題的立場、觀點與看法。

Marketing Manager: When would be the best timing to issue a statement then?

行銷經理：什麼時間點適合發表聲明稿？

1 行銷

2 廣告

3 媒體採購

4 公關公司

5 網路行銷

6 企業社會形象

PR Manager: On the first day, we usually just monitor the media and public reaction. On the second day, if the media are still very much interested, we conduct a contingency meeting for the worst-case scenario (this is where we are now). On the third day, we need to release the brand or company statement to the public. Otherwise, the media will start to make their own assumptions and conclusions based on their own investigation or on uncertified laboratory results. If we do not act by then, not only might the media's conclusions not benefit us, but the media will also complain about our passive attitude. Timing is critical.

公關經理：通常事發的第一天，我們會觀察媒體與大眾的反應；第二天，當媒體持續追蹤且對此議題有興趣，這便是我們需要召開緊急會議來商討最壞情況的對策，這便是我們現在的時間點。在第三天，我們必須對媒體與大眾發表公司或品牌的說法，可以用聲明稿的方式。不然，媒體會開始自行以他們的方式查訪，或自行送到未知單位檢驗，並作出假設或結論，到那個時候，我們不只要擔心檢驗結果是否對我們有利，還得面對媒體對我們消極態度的抱怨。我們千萬不要錯過的重要時間點。

Marketing Manager: Understood. Should we release the statement via email and the website, or we should call a press conference?

行銷經理：了解。我們應該透過電子郵件、網站還是開記者會的方式來發表聲明？

PR Manager: We could just do this via email and website with follow-up calls to the journalists. Our product still meets

公關經理：我們只需要透過電子郵件與網站發表，之後再以電話追蹤的方式確認記

food safety standards and Department of Health regulations. No need to call a press conference to explain anything.

者們都已經收到即可，畢竟這個產品仍然符合國家衛生檢驗單位的食品安全標準，不需要召開記者會說明或解釋任何事。

ABC 有料字彙 Vocabulary

- **olein** (*n.*) [ˋolɪɪn] 油脂；油酸
  The ingredients used in this product include salt, and palm **olein**.
  這產品所用的成份包括鹽及棕櫚油。

- **greasy** (*adj.*) [ˋgrisɪ] 油膩的
  Look at your **greasy** hair!
  看看你那油膩膩的頭髮！

- **advertorial** (*n.*) [ˌædvɝˋtorɪəl] 社論式廣告；主文內廣告
  Advertorials and infomercials are new marketing trends.
  主文內廣告與資訊型廣告是新的行銷趨勢。

- **news release** (*n.*) [njuz] [rɪˋlis] 新聞稿
  The company issues a **news release** to inform the media promptly.
  這公司發布新聞稿迅速地通知媒體。

- **statement** (*n.*) [ˋstetmənt] 聲明；說明；陳述
  He made a public **statement** about the resignation.
  他為辭職發表了公開聲明。

- **clarify** (*v.*) [ˋklærəˌfaɪ] 澄清
  His statement helps **clarify** the situation.
  他的聲明協助釐清情況。

- **timing** (*n.*) [ˋtaɪmɪŋ] 時機
  It's probably not the best **timing** now to reveal the truth.
  現在也許不是揭露事實最好的時機。

- **critical** (*adj.*) [ˋkrɪtɪk!] 關鍵性的
  His **critical** remarks have been a great help.
  他關鍵性的評論幫了很大的忙。

1 行銷

2 廣告

3 媒體採購

4 公關公司

5 網路行銷

6 企業社會形象

有料句型 Sentence Pattern

句型 1 ↘

A ..., while B ...　A 是這樣，而 B 是那樣。

We fry our products, **while** they bake theirs.
我們的產品是用炸的，而他們的產品是用烤的。

Last time we used the images bought from a photo gallery, **while** this time we are going to use the original shots.
上次我們是從圖庫買圖的，這一次我們要用新拍攝的圖。

A news release is to share positive news, **while** a statement is to clarify the brand or company position.
新聞稿是用來分享正面新聞的，而聲明稿是用來澄清品牌或公司的定位。

句型 2 ↘

When..., I would suggest ...　當在⋯的情況下，我會建議⋯。

When a brand is facing a public issue, **I would suggest** issuing a brand statement or company statement.
當品牌在面對公眾議題的情況下，我會建議發表一份品牌聲明稿或公司聲明稿。

When we use an stock image, **I would suggest** to check the licenses provisions carefully.
當我們使用圖庫的圖片時，我會建議仔細確認授權規定。

When it comes to consumer impression, **I would suggest** we pay serious attention on it.
當說到消費者印象的時候，我會建議我們要非常認真看待這件事。

1 行銷

2 廣告

3 媒體採購

4 公關公司

5 網路行銷

6 企業社會形象

When a competitor or media outlet releases negative laboratory results about your brand, and you have no idea what is going on yet, but the journalists are already calling, the basic answer from a brand PR representative should always be "We have to first understand the method, mechanism, and conditions of the experiment, and the quantity and source of the product tested. I will contact you when I have further information." Don't give feedback or a denial too fast, as you may never have a chance to restate.

　　當媒體或競爭對手公佈一份不利的檢驗報告時，有時還來不及了解發生了什麼事，記者們卻已經打電話來了，這時候別急著太快反駁或是回應，以免之後沒機會再重新給另一種說法或解釋，最基本的公關回答是「我們不清楚產品檢驗的方法、過程情況、產品來源與數量，我們會再有進一步訊息時，主動與您聯絡」。

Dialogue 2 　延伸對話

Shift Focus to a New Subject? I Like It! 轉移焦點？我喜歡！

 情境說明 *Situation*

Mitchell and Lucy are working at G Pharmaceutical Company as PR AE, and they are discussing the contents of news release of a new launched cold medicine.

米切爾與露西是 G 製藥公司的公關人員，他們正在討論一款新上市的感冒藥，新聞稿的內容應為何。

♀♂**角色介紹** *Characters*

Mitchell: PR Account Executive
Lucy: PR Account Executive

米切爾：公關專員
露西：公關專員

 情境對話 *Dialogue*

Mitchell: <u>No offense</u>, it's just I personally think <u>it's a big challenge</u> if we are going to build a positive image for a cold medicine.

Lucy: True, I guess we'll need more creativity.

米切爾：沒有冒犯的意思，但是我個人覺得要替感冒藥建立正面印象，是個大挑戰。

露西：的確，我想我們需要更多的創意。

Mitchell: So, if we don't focus on getting cold, but focus on getting better quickly?

米切爾：如果我們不強調感冒這件事，而是強調迅速回復健康這件事呢？

Lucy: <u>Shift focus to a new subject?</u> I like it!

露西：轉移焦點？我喜歡！

Mitchell: Moreover, we should also provide some new knowledge of cold, you know, this makes people feel that our company cares about peoples' health.

米切爾：還有，我們也應該傳達一些感冒新知，妳知道的，這樣可以讓人感覺藥廠在乎國人健康。

Lucy: You are right. It will be great if we can add some research data.

露西：對。如果能添加些研究數據就更棒了。

Mitchell: Can you help in searching this part?

米切爾：這部份可以請妳負責搜尋嗎？

Lucy: Sure.

露西：沒問題。

短句補給 Useful Phrases

✓ No offense. （我）沒有冒犯的意思。

✓ It is a big challenge. 這是個大挑戰。

✓ Shift focus to a new subject. 轉移焦點到新的議題上。

1 行銷

2 廣告

3 媒體採購

4 公關公司

5 網路行銷

6 企業社會形象

We received a consumer complaint from a government official. The official government letter has to be answered, in writing, within 7 days. Meanwhile, the consumer called us today directly, asking for huge compensation. She said if we didn't pay her, she would call the media instead.

我們收到一件從政府機關轉來的消費者投訴，這封官方轉來的公文需要在七天內回覆，不過同時，今天這位消費者已經直接致電給我們，要求高額的賠償金，如果我們無法支付他的話，她打算接著聯絡媒體。

Dialogue 1　主題對話　35

A Complaint Could Become a Crisis If You Don't Handle It Properly.
沒處理好的話，小抱怨可能變成大危機。

情境說明 *Situation*

One consumer filed a complaint to the city government in Taiwan about a horrible live worm found inside a package of our potato chip brand. She is threatening to call all the media tomorrow.

一位消費者向台灣的一個市政府進行申訴，表示發現了一隻可怕又活生生的蟲在我們品牌的洋芋片包裝袋內，她正威脅著要將此事告知媒體。

情境對話 *Dialogue*

Marketing Manager: I don't think we should pay that huge compensation to her. That is encouraging bad behavior. Besides, I don't think our product quality control is so flawed.

PR Manager: I agree. However, we should prevent any negative impact if it goes to the media. First of all, I took some pictures of the product package at issue - and also the worm - when I paid a visit to the consumer. Afterward, I sent the pictures to a well-known entomologist. Even by visual

行銷經理：我不認為我們應該支付高額的賠償金給她，這是在鼓勵一個不對行為，此外，我不認為我們品管會有如此的瑕疵。

公關經理：我同意，但是，我們仍然需要避免媒體的負面影響，我今天拜訪消費者的事後，已經將這產品包裝與蟲體拍了些照片，之後，我將這些照片寄給一個知名的昆蟲學家，光是透過照片

193

examination, the entomologist confirmed this type of worm exists only in Asia, particularly in countries like Taiwan and the Philippines. Also, the worm would die within one hour of staying in a dry environment. Potatoes and potato chips are not food for that type of worm.

Marketing Manager: That is a good point. Our products are all made in, and imported from, the US.

PR Manager: Correct. That is why I asked the entomologist to issue a written certificate about the visual examination—so we could show it to the media when needed.

Marketing Manager: Did the consumer feel ill after eating it? The media love a victim story.

PR Manager: I joined the consumer at the public hospital for a health check. The doctor confirmed the good health of the consumer.

Marketing Manager: What is our

的檢視，這位昆蟲學家表示，這種蟲只存在在亞洲，特別是台灣與菲律賓這樣的國家。並且，如果離水並在乾燥環境超過一個小時，這種蟲是無法存活的，而馬鈴薯或馬鈴薯片都不是這種蟲的主食。

行銷經理：這是一個很好的觀點，我們的產品全部都是由美國進口的。

公關經理：正確，這也是我要找昆蟲學家寫出書面證明的原因，我們可以在必要的時後，將此證明出示給媒體。

行銷經理：消費者在食用後，有任何感到不適嗎？媒體喜歡這一類的受害者故事。

公關經理：是的，我已陪同消費者到公立醫院做了檢查，醫生表示，消費者的健康狀況一切安好。

行銷經理：我們法律上的責

responsibility, legally?

任是什麼？

Legal Manager: According to the Taiwan Consumer Protection Act, the manufacturing company has to compensate the consumer with the value of triple the price of the product if any physical or non-physical damage was caused by using the product.

法務經理：依據台灣消費者保護法，如果產品對消費者造仍任何身體或非身體上的損害，製造商必須以三倍產品的售價賠償之。

PR Manager: The situation as of now is that I brought a gift pack over on the day of my visit. The gift pack value equals the triple the retail price of our product. No damage was caused and no evidence proves the worm was found inside the package.

公關經理：現在的狀況是，我在拜訪消費者時，買了一個禮盒帶過去，那個禮盒的價值等同於三倍產品的市售價格，消費者沒有任何的身體上的損害，也沒有直接的證明該蟲體在包裝開封前即存在包裝內。

1 行銷

2 廣告

3 媒體採購

4 公關公司

5 網路行銷

6 企業社會形象

ABC 有料字彙 Vocabulary

- **threaten** (v.) [ˋθrɛtən] 威脅
  He **threatened** to ruin the show.
  他威脅要毀了這場秀。

- **flaw** (n.) [flɔ] 瑕疵；缺陷
  We find a **flaw** in the product when testing.
  我們測試時發現了產品有瑕疵。

- **impact** (v.) [ɪmˋpækt] 影響；衝擊
  We are eager to know how the price will **impact** on consumer choices.
  我們渴望知道價格將如何衝擊消費者決定。

- **entomologist** (n.)[ˌɛntəˋmɑlədʒɪst] 昆蟲學家
  We have the most famous **entomologist** here to ensure a great insect fair.
  我們請來最有名的昆蟲學家以確保有一場很棒的昆蟲展。

- **import** (v.) [ɪmˋport] 進口
  The feeding stuff is **imported** from America.
  飼料是從美國進口的。

- **victim** (n.) [ˋvɪktɪm] 受害者；犧牲者
  They are the **victims** of that accident.
  他們是那場意外的受害者。

- **triple** (v.) [ˋtrɪp!] 使成三倍
  The sale volume **tripled** after that promotion.
  促銷後的銷售量成長了三倍。

- **physical** (*adj.*) [ˋfɪzɪk!] 身體上的
  This product is designed for those who obsess with **physical** fitness.
  這產品是專為健身上癮的那些人設計的。

- **damage** (*n.*) [ˋdæmɪdʒ] 傷害
  The **damage** to the company's reputation was considerable.
  對那家公司聲譽的傷害是相當可觀的。

- **prove** (*v.*) [pruv] 證明
  The sales volume have **proved** that the strategy works.
  銷售量已經證明了策略奏效。

🐦🐦 有料句型 Sentence Pattern

句型 1 ↘

We should... if it goes to...　假如是牽涉到…情況的話，我們應該…。

We should prevent any negative impact **if it goes to** the media.
假如是牽涉到媒體的話，我們應該避免任何的負面影響。

We should make sure the images are available for commercial use **if it goes to** those stock images.
假如是牽涉到圖庫的圖的話，我們應該確定圖片可供商業用途。

We should build a team **if it goes to** the law.
假如是牽涉到法律的話，我們應該成立一個專案小組。

句型 2 ↘

The media loves ...　媒體總愛…。

The media loves a victim story.
媒體總愛受害者的故事。

The media loves a bloody smell.　They won't go easy on him this time.
媒體就是愛血腥的氣味。他們這次不會輕易放過他。

The media loves to stretch the truth.
媒體總愛誇大事實。

1 行銷

2 廣告

3 媒體採購

4 公關公司

5 網路行銷

6 企業社會形象

Expert Tips
知識補給

　　A consumer complaint could become a huge crisis if you don't handle it properly. Collecting the evidence needed to protect your brand, ensuring medical treatment for the consumer, and completing the legal responsibilities required of a manufacturing company are the three major things to do.

　　消費者抱怨，如果處理不當，可能演變為一個很大的危機。收集相關的證據來保護品牌，並確定消費者的身體損害都得到適當的醫療處理，並且完成製造商應負擔的賠償責任，是面對處理這類事件的三件主要的步驟。

Dialogue 2　延伸對話 36

I Got A Customer Complaint Call... 我接到一通客訴的電話…

 情境說明 *Situation*

Fred got a customer complaint call, and he needs to discuss with Cliff about how to deal with it.

佛雷德接到了一個顧客的客訴電話，他需要和克里夫商量怎麼回應。

♀♂角色介紹 *Characters*

Fred: Customer Relations Manager
Cliff: PR Manager

佛雷德：顧客關係管理經理
克里夫：公關經理

💬 情境對話 *Dialogue*

Fred: Cliff, I am looking for you.	佛雷德：克里夫，我正在找你。
Cliff: What's wrong?	克里夫：怎麼了嗎？
Fred: I got a customer complaint call, and I want to ask you how to deal with it.	佛雷德：我接到一通顧客抱怨的電話，想請問你該怎麼處理？
Cliff: About our clothes or the attitude from staff at the stores?	克里夫：關於我們販售的衣服還是店員態度的？

Fred: It's about the products we sell. She said, there is a hole on it when she went back home and had a careful looking.

佛雷德：是關於商品的。她說，買回家的衣服仔細檢查後發現已經破了一個洞。

Cliff: Not a problem at all. As long as she keeps the clothing tag well, and brings the receipt with her, then goes to any of our stores for change or return.

克里夫：沒問題的。只要吊牌保存完好，攜帶發票回到店內辦理退換貨即可。

Fred: But it seems that she already complained this whole thing on the Internet.

佛雷德：不過她似乎已經在網路上抱怨這件事了。

Cliff: This could be a little bit trouble. OK, please talk with her, and tell her that <u>we'll appreciate it if</u> she can delete the messages. We can offer her some coupons.

克里夫：這就麻煩了。這樣吧，請告訴她，如果她刪除這些留言我們會很感激的。而公司可以提供折價券給她。

短句補給 Useful Phrases

✓ What's wrong? 怎麼了嗎？
✓ How to deal with it? 該怎麼處理？
✓ We'll appreciate it if... 如果是…的話，我們會很感激。

隨著網路發達，企業與個人也就越來越依賴網路。網路行銷類型有哪些？該怎麼在網路上做行銷，以達成更大的知名度或銷售，要當個現代行銷人，你一定不能錯過這個篇章的內容。

5.
網路行銷
Internet Marketing

官網整合
Official Website

We are a big corporation that owns several brands. Each brand has its own website and can have promotional sites as well. The corporate PR manager has to manage multiple websites at the same time. In order to enhance corporate reputation and awareness, we are planning to integrate all the websites into one.

　　我們是一個擁有數個品牌的大公司，而旗下的每個品牌都有自己的官網或活動促銷網頁。身為一個企業公關，我們必須在同時管理幾個網站，為了加強企業的形象與知名度，我們正打算整合所有個別網站。

1 行銷

2 廣告

3 媒體採購

4 公關公司

5 網路行銷

6 企業社會形象

Dialogue 1　主題對話 37

We Are Going to Launch This Site in December!
我們要在十二月啟用這網站！

 情境說明 *Situation*

The corporate PR manager is conducting a meeting to discuss corporate website development. The marketing and PR managers from each brand are all present.

企業公關經理正在召開一個企業網站發展的討論會議，每一個品牌的行銷與公關經理都出席了這個會議。

情境對話 *Dialogue*

Corp PR Manager: We've all acknowledged that there are four different websites in our group. All of the brands on those sites are getting a lot of attention from the public, but this year headquarters wants to develop a corporate platform to let consumers know more about our group.

Manager of Brand A: Understood. So there will be a front page on the corporate website providing links to each brand website?

企業公關經理：我們了解目前我們集團內有四個不同的官網，所有的品牌也都有很高的大眾關注，但是今年度，總部希望發展一個企業官網的平台，將所有的個別品牌納入，讓消費者更了解我們集團。

品牌 A 經理：了解，所以我們還會有一個企業官網的首頁，提供每一個品牌官網的聯結嗎？

Manager of Brand B: <u>When would this platform go live?</u>

品牌 B 經理：這個平台什麼時候上線？

Corp PR Manager: Yes, we will create a front page with the visuals of all brands and also the links. <u>We are targeting to launch</u> this corporate site in December.

企業公關經理：是的，我們會製作這樣一個企業官網首頁，上面有每一個品牌的視覺與連結，我們預計在十二月讓企業網站上線。

Manager of Brand A: What kind of information should we provide to you?

品牌 A 經理：什麼樣的訊息我們應該提供給你？

Corp PR Manager: You need to provide me with all the brand logos and the most updated visuals for quarter 4 by the end of this month. I will also create a page to introduce the history of each brand. Could you provide a brand story in one page or less, and also provide historical visuals?

企業公關經理：你們需要在月底前，給我所有品牌標誌，與第四季的最新視覺，另外，你們可以提供品牌故事與品牌歷史圖嗎？

Manager of Brand C: Sure. We could do that. What is the agency you are using for website design? I am worried about the tone and manner of the brand history page.

品牌 C 經理：當然，我們可以這個做，我們是用哪一種廠商來設計我們的官網，我有點擔心設計的風格會與我們的品牌有些出入。

Manager of Brand B: And beyond the design, I would also suggest the font size of the brand history page should similar to

品牌 B 經理：不只是設計風格，我建議品牌故事的字體大小，也應該與我們的品

our brand page.

牌網頁一致化。

Corp PR Manager: Are there any requests for special functions?

企業公關經理：還有沒有其他的特殊功能的需求？

Manager of Brand B: I would like to have a download page for media journalists to download all our product visuals and news releases. It's similar to a member login function. That way we could save time by not having to send visuals of our products via email. Also it could help avoid the "traffic jam" created by sending large emails.

品牌 B 經理：我想要有一個媒體下載區，可以讓記者們下載所有的產品圖與新聞稿，這有點類似會員專區，且有登入的功能，我們可以因此省下時間透過電子郵件來寄圖檔，也可以避免大容量的電子信件引起的網路擁塞。

ABC 有料字彙 Vocabulary

- **platform** (n.) [`plæt,fɔrm] 平台
  The company provides a **platform** for people to express their opinions.
  這家公司提供了一個可以表達意見的平台。

- **link** (v.) [lɪŋk] 連結
  The problem is how we **link** the logo to the product.
  問題是我們如何將商標圖案和產品做連結。

- **go live** [go `laɪv] 上線
  The system will **go live** soon.
  這系統即將上線。

- **launch** (*v.*) [lɔntʃ] 開辦；開始從事（某事）
  The two brothers **launched** a new business.
  這兩兄弟開始了一個新事業。

- **font** (*n.*) [fɑnt] （電腦）字型；字體
  You can customize the **font** and select from several languages.
  你可以自訂字型並自多種語言中選取。

- **login** (*v.*) [lɑg`ɪn] 登入；進入系統
  Just enter the account name and password to **login**.
  只要鍵入帳號、密碼就可以登入。

- **jam** (*n.*) [dʒæm] 擁擠；堵塞
  They were stuck in a traffic **jam** on their way to the road show.
  他們在往巡迴演出的路上遇上塞車了。

有料句型 Sentence Pattern

句型 1 ↘

go live (v.) （電腦系統）測試完成並上線

go-live (adj.)

When would this website **go live**?
這個網站何時上線？

They are going to announce the **go-live** date this week.
他們將會在本週宣布上線日期。

User acceptance testing is key for a new system to **go-live**.
使用者接受度測試是新系統上線的關鍵。

1 行銷

2 廣告

3 媒體採購

4 公關公司

5 網路行銷

6 企業社會形象

句型 2 ↘

We are targeting to...　我們打算要… / 我們目標是…

We are targeting to launch this corporate site in December.
我們打算要在十二月讓企業網站上線。

We are targeting to become one of the Top 10 suppliers in the world by the end of the year.
我們的目標是要在年底躋身世界十大供應商之列。

We are targeting to a 10% increase in sales this year.
我們今年的目標是增加百分之十的銷售量。

Expert Tips
知識補給

Usually when planning website development, we will register a few website addresses which have names similar to our brand. These addresses redirect to our brand. The registration cost is low, and having them all registered under our control could prevent future abuse by others.

通常在計劃一個網站發展時，我們會註冊幾個與公司名雷同的網址名，或是與品牌類似的網址名，這些註冊費用不高，但是可以避免未來這些類似的網址被不肖業者所濫用。

Dialogue 2　延伸對話 38

Will It Create Clash Feeling to Customers?
會讓顧客感覺到衝突嗎？

 情境說明 *Situation*

Sheena and Mark are discussing how to integrate the websites under the company's name.

席娜和馬克正在商量該怎麼將公司旗下的網站整合。

♀♂ **角色介紹** *Characters*

Sheena: PR Account Executive
Mark: IT Account Executive

席娜：公關專員
馬克：資訊部專員

 情境對話 *Dialogue*

Sheena: Hi, Mark. May I speak with you for few minutes?

Mark: Sure. Wow, Sheena, you are looking really great.

Sheena: I just keep early hours. Right, I am wondering how are things going with official website integration?

Mark: Only half way. To be honest, I have some doubts.

席娜：嗨，馬克。我可以耽誤你幾分鐘時間嗎？

馬克：沒問題。哇，席娜，妳看起來氣色真好。

席娜：我只是早睡早起罷了。對了，我想問你官網整合得怎麼樣了？

馬克：才進行到一半而已呢。老實說，我也有點疑問。

Sheena: What are they?

Mark: I want to know if we should move the past campaign homepage to a new area, or put under the related brand's website?

Sheena: I have to ask my boss about this. Is there anything else?

Mark: Yes. Since the company doesn't want consumers know that certain brands are belonging to us when some brands started. You know, the company has history and there are some new brands are pursuing trends and rich in variety.

Sheena: You are afraid that if we put them together, will create clash feeling to customers. Well, I have to ask my boss, too.

Mark: I see, then I suggest our two departments should have a meeting together.

席娜：是什麼呢？

馬克：我想知道過往的活動網頁，應該另外放一個區塊，還是放在對應的品牌網頁裡面？

席娜：這個我要請教我的主管了。還有嗎？

馬克：有。因為當初有些品牌成立之初，公司並不想讓消費者知道這是公司的品牌，妳知道的，公司本身有歷史，而新品牌有些是訴求新潮與活潑。

席娜：你是怕放在一起會給消費者衝突感？恐怕這也得請問我的主管了。

馬克：這樣的話，我建議兩個部門開會討論吧。

短句補給 Useful Phrases

✓ May I speak with you for few minutes? 我可以耽誤你幾分鐘嗎？

✓ You are looking really great. 你看起來氣色真好。

✓ I just keep early hours. 我一般都早睡早起。

211

社群網站
Social Media

Digital marketing includes owned media, paid media, and earned media. If a marketing strategy does not include digital marketing, it will not make an adequate impression in the daily life of the consumer.

一般的網路行銷分成三種：自有媒體、付費媒體與口碑媒體。行銷策略如果不考慮到網路行銷，也其實根本無法進入消費者的日常生活。

1 行銷

2 廣告

3 媒體採購

4 公關公司

5 網路行銷

6 企業社會形象

Dialogue 1　主題對話

More and More Investment in Digital Channels.
對數位媒體的投資越來越多了。

情境說明 *Situation*

The marketing manager is trying to convince the general manager to invest more in digital channels.

行銷經理正在試著說服總經理，關於進一步的投資網路媒體管道。

情境對話 *Dialogue*

Marketing Manager: In the past, we invested in digital media buys such as banners and key word searches. This year, we are focusing more on PPC (pay per click) and SEO (search engine optimization), and also social media management. Social media is a part of owned media. Usually, we use the company official website to provide product or brand information and use social media as a conversation hub to engage with consumers; we use company e-mail as an extension of customer service and use mobile applications as a membership program system.

行銷經理：在過去，我們會投資一些網路媒體購買，如看版、或關鍵字等，近幾年來，我們較著重在點擊付費與搜尋引擎優化，以及社群網路的管理。社群網站是我們的自有媒體，一般來說，我們會運用官網來提供產品或品牌資訊，並運用社群網站來與消費者進行對話，來達到與消費者接觸、互動的目的，並運用公司的電子郵件信箱作為提供服務的延伸，運用手機的軟體為招募會員系統。

213

General Manager: How can social media engage consumers in a way the website can't?

總經理：為何一個社群網站可以與消費者接觸、互動，而一個網站卻不能？

Marketing Manager: The brand actually can use social media to interact with consumers instead of traditional one-way communication. Besides, since social media is not the official website, it can show more personality and brand character to build the relationship with consumers, and reduce the gap between the brand and consumers. However, feedback from the brand has to be provided promptly. Within 24 hours is suggested. Otherwise, consumers will see it as a disrespectful gesture.

行銷經理：品牌通常可以透過社群網站與消費者進行雙向對話，而傳統的網站卻只是單向的溝通。此外，由於社群網站不是一個官方網站，它可以表現多一點個性與品牌特色，來與消費者建立關係，並拉近品牌與消費者之間的距離，但是，所以品牌的回覆必須要及時，建議要在二十四小時內，否則消費者會認為品牌不重視他們的聲音。

General Manager: How could the mobile APP become a membership program system?

總經理：手機軟體是如何變成會員招募系統的呢？

Marketing Manager: During installation of an APP, the login process could collect consumer personal data, such as name, email address and other information. That is exactly what we do when recruiting a member.

行銷經理：當下載一個手機軟體時，通常註冊的過程，會收集到消費者的個人資訊，如姓名、電子郵件或其他資訊，這即是當我們要招募會員時會做的。

1 行銷

2 廣告

3 媒體採購

4 公關公司

5 網路行銷

6 企業社會形象

General Manager: I wonder what is the KPI (key performance indicator) to evaluate social media?

Marketing Manager: We can check the numbers on sharing, likes, comments, time spent, clicks, contest entries, and so on.

General Manager: What is "social listening" about?

Marketing Manager: "Social Listening" is a tool for us to define who the influencers are and to spread messages effectively by observing the online behavior of our consumers.

總經理：我在想，評估社群網站經營的績效的主要指標會是什麼？

行銷經理：我們會視分享的數字、喜歡次數、留言、停留時間、點擊次數、活動參與次數、與訂閱數字來評估。

總經理：什麼是「社群傾聽」？

行銷經理：「社群傾聽」是一個網路觀察系統，讓我們了解哪些族群具影響力且可以有效散播訊息。

ABC 有料字彙 Vocabulary

- **adequate** (*adj.*) [ˋædəkwɪt] 足夠的；足量的
  We don't have **adequate** information to increase investment.
  我們沒有足夠的資訊增加投資金額。

- **engage** (*v.*) [ɪnˋgedʒ] 使從事；使忙於
  He was **engaged** in the yearly project recently.
  他最近忙於那件年度企劃。

- **extension** (*n.*) [ɪkˋstɛnʃən] 延伸
  May I have an **extension** to finish my project?
  我可以有多點（延伸的）時間來完成我的案子嗎？

- **interact** (*v.*) [ˌɪntəˋrækt] 互動
  The host **interacts** well with other guests in that show.
  主持人在表演中與其他來賓互動良好。

- **disrespectful** (*adj.*) [ˌdɪsrɪˋspɛktfəl] 無理的；失禮的
  You are accused of being **disrespectful** at the party last night.
  你在昨晚的派對中被指稱失禮。

- **installation** (*n.*) [ˌɪnstəˋleʃən] 安裝；裝置設備
  All you need is three minutes to finish the **installation**.
  你需要的只是花個三分鐘的時間來安裝。

- **recruit** (*v.*) [rɪˋkrut] 徵募、吸收（新成員）
  Most of the performers are **recruited** from professional theatrical troupes.
  大部分的表演者是從專業劇團找來的。

- **define** (*v.*) [dɪˋfaɪn] 為⋯下定義
  The brand preference is about how you **define** yourself.
  品牌偏好和一個人如何定義自己有關係。

🐤🐤 有料句型 *Sentence Pattern*

句型 1 ↘

To..., ... has to be provided promptly. 為了⋯，必須快速提供⋯。

To build the relationship with consumers, feedback from the brand **has to be provided promptly.**
為了建立與消費者間的關係，品牌必須快速做出回應

To manage a crisis, a formal company statement **has to be provided promptly.**
要處理危機，務必快速提供一份正式的公司聲明稿。

To clarify the situation, an overall investigation report **has to be provided promptly.**

要釐清現況，必須立即提供一份全面性的調查報告。

句型 2 ↘

Otherwise, consumers will see it as... 否則（不然的話），消費者會認為…

Otherwise, consumers will see it as a disrespectful gesture.

否則，消費者會把它看做是不受重視的表現。

Otherwise, consumers will see them as luxury goods, not necessities.

否則，消費者會把它們看做是奢侈品，而非必需品。

Otherwise, consumers will see it as an outdated product.

否則，消費者會認為這是過時的產品。

Expert Tips
知識補給

Gaining a comprehensive view of online conversations about the brand and also cultivating the conversation to amplify the positive buzz is the key. Plus, integrating key platforms to create a more seamless experience for consumers can affect brand preference and loyalty.

取得全方位的角度，來觀察網路關於品牌的對話，並適當的調整對話內容，讓正面的話題與影響留在網路是一個重點，此外，整合所有重點平台，提供消費者一個完美的經驗，藉以提升品牌的喜好度與忠誠度。

Dialogue 2　延伸對話

How's the Effectiveness of the Advertisement on Social Networks?
社交網站廣告的成效如何？

 情境說明 *Situation*

William is bothered by whether he should suggest the company to put advertisement on social networkson not, He thinks of Kate, and decides to call her.

威廉正為是否要建議公司在社群網站上刊登廣告的事情煩惱，剛好他想起了凱特，於是決定打電話給她。

♀♂ **角色介紹** *Characters*

William: PR Account Executive of F Company
Kate: Assistant Manager of H Advertising Agency

威廉：F 公司公關專員
凱特：H 廣告公司副理

 情境對話 *Dialogue*

William: Hi, my old school friend. <u>It has been a long time.</u>

威廉：老同學，好久不見。

Kate: Right, and <u>you should hang out with us more.</u> So, what's up?

凱特：是呀，你應該多和我們一起出來玩才對。找我有事嗎？

William: I am just wondering how is the effectiveness of your company's advertisement on social networks?

威廉：我想請教一下，妳們公司在社交網站上的廣告成效如何？

Kate: It's pretty good, actually.

凱特：還不錯，真的。

William: I see. I am more curious about how to evaluate it?

威廉：是唷。我比較好奇你們如何評估。

Kate: We focused on average click through rate and conversion, and the sales grew fifteen percentages than last month.

凱特：我們公司是看計算點選率和實際成交的轉換率。業績也比上個月成長了15%。

William: That's worth trying then.

威廉：那就值得一試。

Kate: Good luck to you!

凱特：祝你好運囉！

短句補給 Useful Phrases

✓ It has been a long time.　好久不見。
✓ You should hang out with us more.　你應該多和我們一起出來。
✓ That's worth trying.　值得一試。

1 行銷

2 廣告

3 媒體採購

4 公關公司

5 網路行銷

6 企業社會形象

電子商務
e-Commerce

E-Commerce is another selling channel in this digital world. Over 65% of people in Taiwan have experienced online shopping. This is a trend, and online shopping will become more and more accessible.

電子商務是網路世界裡的另一種的銷售管道，超過百分之六十五的台灣民眾曾經嘗試過線上購物，這是一個趨勢，網路線上購物會變得越來越容易。

1 行銷

2 廣告

3 媒體採購

4 公關公司

5 網路行銷

6 企業社會形象

Dialogue 1　主題對話 41

Over 65% of People in Taiwan Have Experienced Online Shopping.
在台灣，百分之六十五的人嘗試過線上購物。

 情境說明 Situation

The company is developing a web-ordering system. The IT specialist and project manager are now discussing with the marketing manager the requirements for the upcoming months.

公司正要開發網路購物系統，IT 部門的專員、行銷經理與專案經理正在討論未來幾個月的需求。

情境對話 Dialogue

Project Manager: Today is the kick-off meeting for the project. We are planning to launch this web-ordering site in 2015. This is an adaptation process, not a creation process. We will adapt the Singapore web-ordering design and translate it into Mandarin. The visual design will be assigned to the marketing team and your advertising agency, but the advertising agency has to cooperate with the IT team to ensure firewall protection and security.

專案經理：今天是這個專案的第一次會議。我們計劃在 2015 年推出這個線上購物網站，這會是一個套用採納的過程，不會是一個從無到有的製作過程，因為我們將套用新加坡的網路線上購物系統設計，並將其翻譯成為中文。視覺的設計會由行銷部的團隊和你們的廣告公司，但是這廣告公司有需要與 IT 團隊合作，來確認防火牆的保護與安全性。

IT Specialist: The Asia regional office has sent me a security checklist for the advertising agency. If the agency meets the criteria, then they will have to sign a confidentiality contract.

Marketing Manager: No problem. I will talk to the agency and make sure they can fulfill the criteria.

Project Manager: Other than that, we need all the product pictures with standard size, file format, and white background. I will send you the standards after this meeting.

Marketing Manager: I understand. However, there are some new products of which we don't have product shots. We have to schedule some time to shoot and retouch them. When do you need those pictures?

Project Manager: The latest date to submit them is the end of this month. Please try to meet the deadline.

Marketing Manager: Sure.

Project Manager: Another thing we need to discuss in the next meeting is the payment terms. Are we going to accept

IT 專員：亞太區的辦公室已經寄給我一份安全檢查清單，用來檢視廣告公司。如果廣告公司符合這些條件，他們之後必須簽署一份保密合約。

行銷經理：沒問題，我會與廣告公司說明，並確保他們能符合公司的條件。

專案經理：除此之外，我們需要所有產品的照片，這些照片得符合標準的大小、尺寸、檔案格式，並且都是白色的背景，我會在會議後寄給你這些照片標準。

行銷經理：我了解，不過有些新產品，我們還沒有它們的產品照，我們必須安排時間重新拍攝或是修片，請問你什麼時候需要這些照片？

專案經理：最遲在這個月底前，得收齊這些照片。請試著在截止日前交出。

行銷經理：當然。

專案經理：在下一次的會議中，我們需要討論一下的事會是付款方式，我們要接受

5 網路行銷　5-3 電子商務

1 行銷

2 廣告

3 媒體採購

4 公關公司

5 網路行銷

6 企業社會形象

credit cards and coupon usage, or only payment on delivery? Currently, the coupons don't have any serial numbers. If we accept those coupons online, how do we identify them?

信用卡付費與折價券的使用嗎？或者是只接受貨物送抵後付款？目前折價券並未印上流水編號，如果我們要在線上接受它，要如何識別呢？

Marketing Manager: I suggest that we should discuss those issues with the finance department next time.

行銷經理：我建議下一次討論這類議題，我們需要找財務部門的人參加。

ABC 有料字彙 Vocabulary

- **kick off** (n.) [kɪk ɔf] 開始；踢掉；趕走。kick-off meeting 專案啟動會議
  Wow! That was an incredible **kick off**.
  哇! 那真是個不可思議的開球。

- **accessible** (adj.) [əkˋsɛsəb!] 易接近的；易取得的，平易近人的
  The internet makes customers personal information **accessible**.
  網路讓客戶資料易於取得。

- **criteria** (n.) [kraɪˋtɪrɪən] 標準；準則
  What **criteria** do customers use when making the purchase decisions?
  顧客在做購買決定時的標準是什麼呢？

- **confidentiality** (n.) [͵kɑnfɪ͵dɛnʃɪˋælɪtɪ] 機密
  The relationship between us is based on **confidentiality**.
  我們之間的關係建立在機密性之上。

- **submit** (*v.*) [səb`mɪt] 使服從，呈交
  All applications must be **submitted** by Friday.
  所有的申請文件都必須在週五呈交。

- **coupon** (*n.*) [`kupɑn] 優待
  The **coupon** entitles you to 10% off your next purchase.
  這張優待券能讓您下次消費抵免 10%的金額。

- **serial** (*adj.*) [ˈsɪriəl] 連續的；一系列的
  Key in the serial numbers and you can join the weekly draw.
  鍵入序號即可參加每週一次的抽獎。

🐤🐤 有料句型 *Sentence Pattern*

句型 1 ↘

I will... and make sure... 我會…並確定…。

I will talk to the agency **and make sure** they can fulfill the criteria.
我會與廣告公司說明，並確保他們能符合公司的條件。

I will do exactly what you just said **and make sure** James also gets your message.
我會照您的吩附去辦，並確定詹姆士也收到您的留言。

I will contact the studio **and make sure** everything is on the right track on the shooting day.
我會連絡工作室，並確定他們拍攝當天一切就緒。

句型 2 ↘

I will... after this meeting.　會議之後，我會...

I will send you the standards **after this meeting.**
會議之後，我會寄出這些標準給您。

I will contact the photographer **after this meeting.**
會議之後，我會連絡攝影師。

I will put the contact list on your desk **after this meeting**.
會議之後，我會將聯絡人名單放您桌上。

Expert Tips
知識補給

An adaptation process for a website is much easier than creating a new site from scratch. If it is a Greater China project, one thing to remember is to mind the text font setting and code of Traditional Chinese.

　　一個網站的套用採納的過程，遠比一個從無到有製作新網站的過程來得容易多，如果這是一個大中華區的案子，需要注意到的便是繁體中文的編碼與字體的設定。

Dialogue 2　延伸對話　42

Let's Say a Group Buying Campaign? 辦團購吧？

情境說明 *Situation*

Becky and Russell run a camera shop together, and now they are discussing how to host a group buying campaign on the Internet.

貝琪和羅素一起經營相機專賣店，兩人正在討論該如何在網路上辦團購活動。

♀♂角色介紹 *Characters*

Becky: The owner of a camera shop
Russell: Becky's husband

貝琪：相機專賣店擁有者
羅素：貝琪的先生

💬情境對話 *Dialogue*

Becky: It's really awful that our last month's sales volume had fallen to the bottom.

Russell: It's been a long time since we held an event on our Fan page on Facebook. Maybe we should try it again.

Becky: You are quite right about this.　But I am wondering what kind of promotion event we should hold?

貝琪：真糟糕，上個月的銷售量低到不能再低了。

羅素：我們好久沒有在臉書的粉絲頁上做活動了。或許我們應該再試試。

貝琪：你說得對。但是，該舉辦什麼活動好呢？

Russell: Let's say a group buying campaign?

羅素：就辦團購吧。

Becky: Perhaps we provide some outdoor sporting goods as a choice, too?

貝琪：也許搭配一些戶外運動商品也不錯？

Russell: We have to purchase them in addition, so forget about it.

羅素：這些商品還要另外採購，算了吧。

Becky: Is it long enough if the group buying continues for three weeks?

貝琪：團購時間有 3 週，夠長嗎？

Russell: I think so. Don't forget it, it's better to allow buyers come to pick the goods up at our shop, so we can save the delivery fees.

羅素：夠了吧。別忘了，最好讓買家到我們店裡領取，還可以省下快遞費呢。

短句補給 Useful Phrases

✓ Have(has) fallen to the bottom.　跌到谷底。
✓ You are quite right about this.　你是對的。
✓ Forget about it.　算了吧。

5-4

電子商務會員
e-Commerce Members

Rookie
菜鳥心聲

Our brand started using a CRM (Customer Relationship Management) program last year, and we have used the CRM database to engage with consumers/customers ever since. People say the CRM database is the most valuable asset and saves costs for the brand.

我們的品牌剛剛從去年開始使用客戶關係管理系統，之後我們也使用了系統內的客戶資料來與消費者接洽，很多人說客戶資料是最有價值的資產，且也會為品牌省下很多的經費。

5 網路行銷　5-4 電子商務會員

1 行銷

2 廣告

3 媒體採購

4 公關公司

5 網路行銷

6 企業社會形象

Dialogue 1　主題對話　43

People Is the Most Valuable Asset! 人，是最有價值的資產！

☕ 情境說明 *Situation*

The marketing team is planning to use CRM data for a contest invitation. Now the CRM supervisor and the marketing manager are having a meeting to discuss the next step.

行銷部正在計劃使用客戶資料來進行一個有獎活動的邀約，目前客戶關係主任正在針對下一步，與行銷經理進行會議討論。

💬 情境對話 *Dialogue*

CRM Supervisor: We now have nearly 30,000 members. We can send event invitations through short cellphone messages. But we can't really send out 30,000 invitations, as there is missing data.

Marketing Manager: How many members in the database have valid cellphone numbers?

CRM Supervisor: I would say maybe 80% of them, based on last time we sent SMS messages in January. Plus, some new members didn't provide cellphone numbers.

Marketing Manager: I see, how about valid

客戶關係主任：我們有近三萬名的會員，我們可以透過手機系統寄發邀請簡訊，然而我們無法寄發三萬通簡訊，因為有些資料的短缺。

行銷經理：有多少位會員在系統中，留下有效的手機號碼？

客戶關係主任：我認為大約百分之八十，這是根據上一次在一月份的簡訊發送記錄。此外，有些新加入的會員，根本未留下手機號碼。

行銷經理：我知道了，那麼

e-mail addresses? We use the e-mail address as the registration name; therefore, all members should have e-mail addresses. The valid email addresses should be more than cell phone numbers.

CRM supervisor: That is true. The mail open rate is only 30% according to the last time we sent promotional e-mail to all members.

Marketing Manager: When is our monthly newsletter issue date? The newsletter open rate is much higher than for promotional e-mail, I think.

CRM Supervisor: Yes, the newsletter will be issued next week. Now is the final proof reading period. You may have to contact the communication team to tell them you want to insert this contest message. It could be very interesting if we insert an article to promote our campaign under the winner's name from the last contest.

Marketing Manager: I don't think it's a good idea to use the winner's name due to

有效的電子郵件地址呢？我們系統是用電子郵件地址來當註冊帳號名稱的，因此，所有的會員應該都留有電子郵件地址，數量應該會比手機號碼較多。

客戶關係主任：這倒是，但是廣告電子信件的開啟閱讀率僅僅只有百分之三十，這是根據上一次，我們用電子信件地址寄送促銷內容給所有會員時的數字。

行銷經理：我們什麼時候發送每個月的電子刊物？我想電子刊物的開信率應該會比促銷廣告信來得高。

客戶關係主任：是的，電子刊物將在下週發行。現在是最後的審閱期，你可能要與公關的團隊問一下，並告訴他們你想將這樣的訊息安插進去。如果我們安排一篇稿子，使用上期有獎活動的得主的名義，大大的推銷這一期的新活動，這應該會很有趣。

行銷經理：我不認為這是個好建議，因為用了得獎者的

data privacy issues. Any information that could identify a person, such as name, photos, telephone numbers, e-mail addresses, mailing addresses, and even preferences, is protected by the government's data privacy policy.

名義，得考慮個人資料保護法的問題。任何資料只要可以分辨出個人，如姓名、照片、電話、電子信箱地址、郵寄地址，甚至是個人習慣偏好，都是在政府的個人資料保護法的規範中。

有料字彙 Vocabulary

- **database** (n.) [ˋdetəˌbes] 資料庫
  The **database** crashed for two hours because of a tiny error.
  資料庫因為一個小小的錯誤當機了兩個小時。

- **registration** (n.) [ˌrɛdʒɪˋstreʃən] 註冊；登記
  You need to provide your cellphone number to complete the **registration**.
  你需要提供手機號碼以完成註冊程序。

- **valid** (adj.) [ˋvælɪd] 有效的
  The password is still **valid**.
  密碼仍然是有效的。

- **promotional** (adj.) [prəˋmoʃən!] 促銷的
  We made a **promotional** video for our product.
  我們為產品做了一個促銷的影片。

- **issue** (v.) [ˋɪʃʊ] 發行
  She **issued** a statement denying everything she was accused of.

- **insert** (v.) [ɪnˋsɝt] 插入
  Do you know how to **insert** a line to a Word document?
  你知道要怎麼在 Word 文件中插入一條線嗎？

· **identify** (*v.*) [aɪˋdɛntəˌfaɪ] 認出；識別
Please identify yourself!
請表明身分！

🐤🐤 有料句型 *Sentence Pattern*

句型 1 ↘

I would say..., based on... 我認為…，基於…（的理由）。

I would say maybe 80% of them, **based on** last time we sent SMS messages in January.
我認為也許是百分之八十，基於上次一月份時我們寄送的簡訊。

I would say an extra back-up plan is needed, **based on** the various situations.
我認為額外的備案是需要的，基於這多變的情況。

I would say pink, **based on** the potential customers we have are teenage girls.
我會選粉紅色，基於我們潛在客戶為青少女的理由。

句型 2 ↘

The ... rate is... according to... （某事件）百分比為… 根據…

The mail open **rate is** only 30% **according to** the last time we sent promotional e-mail to all members.
廣告郵件的開啟閱讀率僅僅只有百分之三十，這是根據上一次，我們用電子信件地址寄送促銷內容給所有會員時的數字。

5 網路行銷　5-4 電子商務會員

1 行銷

2 廣告

3 媒體採購

4 公關公司

5 網路行銷

6 企業社會形象

The click-through **rate is** increased **according to** the latest page counter with statistics.

根據最新的網頁計數器統計數字，點擊率增加了。

Basically, the reason a brand would have a CRM program is to retain the consumer's loyalty, engage with consumers, and track consumers' preferences. Ultimately, CRM allows brands to better manage, serve, and extract value from consumers/customers while improving operational efficiency—something that is critical in today's service industry.

基本上，品牌會建立一個客戶關係管理系統，就是想維護消費者的忠誠度、與消費者多些互動，並且追蹤消費者的喜好，最終的目的，這個系統可幫助品牌管理、服務，或者從改善營運流程中從消費者的回應得到更高的價值，這也是在現今服務業的環境裡很重要的一環。

Dialogue 2　延伸對話　◎44

Our Customers Care More About… 客戶更在意的是…

 情境說明 *Situation*

Luke and Titan met each other before the morning meeting, and they are talking about how to provide more service to online members.

路克與泰坦在部門的晨會開始之前遇見了彼此，他們正討論著如何提供更多服務給網路會員。

♀♂ **角色介紹** *Characters*

Luke: Customer Service Manager
Titan: Marketing Manager

路克：顧客服務經理
泰坦：行銷經理

 情境對話 *Dialogue*

Luke: Hi, Titan, have you heard that U Airline decided to out of the market last week?

Titan: So I have been told.

Luke: It's terrible, isn't it? I heard that's because they cannot catch the wave of online marketing.

路克：嗨，泰坦。你聽說 U 航空公司上週決定退出市場？

泰坦：我聽說了。

路克：挺嚇人的，不是嗎？聽說就是栽在跟不上網路行銷的浪潮。

1 行銷

2 廣告

3 媒體採購

4 公關公司

5 網路行銷

6 企業社會形象

Titan: What are you trying to say then?

Luke: Since most of the ticket booking comes from the Internet, maybe we need to offer more mileage points, more promotion events, and VIP services.

Titan: For example, what kind of VIP services?

Luke: Such as, book a ticket during a certain period of time, then the consumer can enjoy the spa massage before boarding.

Titan: But the research shows that our customers appreciate the realistic discount.

Luke: Then we offer more discount, however, for the next time online booking use.

泰坦：你有何高見嗎？

路克：既然大多數訂票來自網路，或許我們應該提高網路訂票的積分、更多促銷活動，以及 VIP 服務。

泰坦：例如哪些 VIP 服務呢？

路克：例如，特定期間上網訂票可以享受登機前的 SPA 按摩。

泰坦：但是調查顯示，我們的客戶更在意實質的折扣。

路克：那麼我們就給予更多的折扣，但是限下次網路訂票時使用。

情境對話 Dialogue

✓ So I have been told.　我聽說了。

✓ It's terrible, isn't it?　挺糟糕的，不是嗎？

✓ Catch the wave of...　抓住⋯的浪潮。

現在的企業可不能只顧營利，也需要花更多時間、金錢在回饋社會的層面。這個篇章帶你了解企業執行公益活動的各方面項。

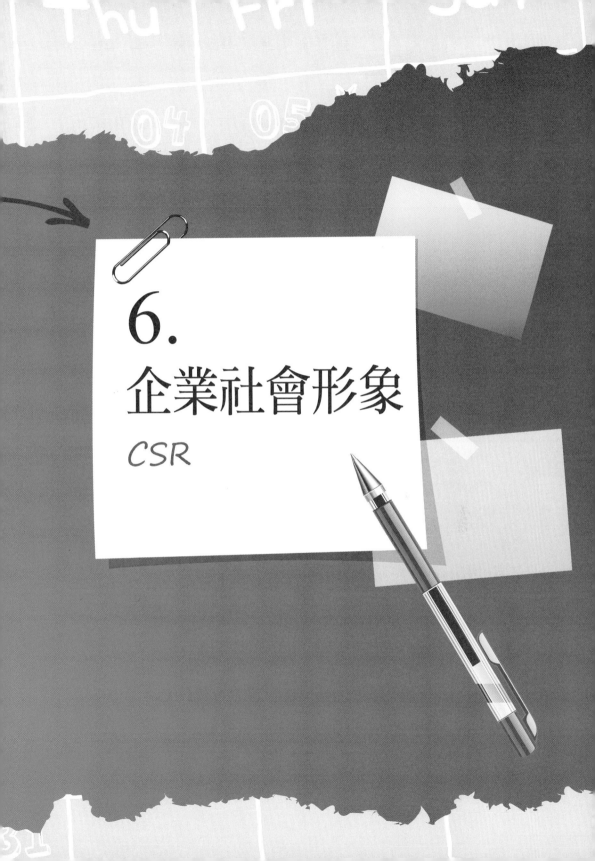

6.
企業社會形象
CSR

品牌活動贊助
Sponsorship

One of the KPIs (Key Performance Indicators) for a PR team is sponsorship program deployment. Usually the negotiation period will be a little longer if it's done in cooperation with the government.

對公關團隊來說，其中一個主要績效指標便是品牌活動贊助的施行。如果是與政府機關的贊助活動合作，那麼通常談判的過程會比較冗長。

1 行銷

2 廣告

3 媒體採購

4 公關公司

5 網路行銷

6 企業社會形象

Dialogue 1　主題對話 45

Where Would Our Brand Logo Be If We Sponsor Your in All That?
如果我們贊助這些的話，我們的 Logo 會放在哪裡呢？

 情境說明 *Situation*

The National Concert Hall is planning to host the International Art Festival of 2014 from months ago. We are already a little too late to contact them now for the sponsorship. And, we have to sponsor some culture-related programs to fulfill the company CSR (Corporate Social Responsibility) annual target.

國家表演廳已經從幾個月前就開始籌辦 2014 國際藝術節，我們現在與他們連繫已經有點遲了。不過，我們得贊助這些文化類的活動，來達到公司企業社會責任的年度目標。

情境對話 *Dialogue*

PR Manager: For us as a European brand, it would be an honor if we could sponsor the festival. We've learned that you already have a few sponsors. Which parts of the festival still need sponsorship?

Concert Hall Specialist: There are a few areas in which we could still use sponsorship, such as ticket printing, the installation of flags on lampposts, the renting of lampposts, and the printing of

公關經理：對我們身為一個歐洲的品牌，如果可以贊助這個藝術節，這會是我們的榮幸。

國家表演廳專員：目前有幾個部分，我們還未找到贊助商，比如票券的印製、街燈旗幟的安裝，街燈柱的租賃費、節目單的印製等等。你

show notes etc. You could imagine it as a package.

PR Manager: I see. Where would our brand logo be if we sponsor you in all that?

Concert Hall Specialist: Of course, your brand logo would be shown on all the tickets, show notes, and flags.

PR Manager: Can our logo be shown on all your communication materials, as we are one of your sponsors for the show — not just on the items we pay for?

Concert Hall Specialist: I understand. That is a fair question to ask. However, there is only one month before the festival. Almost all the materials like promotion ads, Internet communication, and invitations are out. That is why we are not able to print your brand name on them.

PR Manager: Right. Given that, how much is the cost of sponsorship for the items you mentioned?

可以把上述這些當成是一個專案的贊助內容。

公關經理：我了解了，那麼如果我們接受這個專案的內容，我們品牌的標誌會被放在哪裡？

國家表演廳專員：當然你們的品牌標識會出現在所有的入場票券、旗幟，及節目單上。

公關經理：是否有可能我們的品牌標識出現在所有製作物上？畢竟我們也算是你們活動的贊助商與協辦單位之一，而不是只出現在我們現在要印製的物品上。

國家表演廳專員：我理解，這當然是應該的部分。然而因為時間的關係，再過一個月藝術節就要展開，幾乎所有的製作物，如宣傳廣告、網路廣告、邀請卡等都早已經出去了，這也是為什麼我已經無法放你們的品牌標識在所有製作物上。

公關經理：是，既然這樣，請問一下您提到的贊助費用是需要多少呢？

6 企業社會形象　6-1 品牌活動贊助

1 行銷

2 廣告

3 媒體採購

4 公關公司

5 網路行銷

6 企業社會形象

Concert Hall Specialist: The original package is about 500K. And yet, we are considering lowering the price, as we cannot print your logo onto all the other materials. How about 300K for the package, plus, you could get 50 free tickets in the VIP area?

PR Manager: Can I know how many copies you will print of the tickets, show notes, and flags in total so we can estimate the exposure numbers?

Concert Hall Specialist: No problem. It's around 100,000 copies. I will send you the actual numbers and information later.

PR Manager: That sounds good. Please also send me the contract at your earliest convenience.

國家表演廳專員：這個專案本來的贊助費用需要五十萬元，但是，由於我們無法印上你們品牌的標識在所有製作物上，我們願意將費用降低一些。如果費用是三十萬元，另外加上五十張貴賓席的入場券？

公關經理：請問需要印製的入場票券、節目單與旗幟的總數為何？我們來評估一下可能曝光露出的數字？

國家表演廳專員：沒問題，總數大約十萬份，我會將具體的數字稍後寄給你。

公關經理：這聽起來很不錯，方便的話，請儘速一起將合約寄給我。

ABC 有料字彙 Vocabulary

• **festival** (*n.*) [ˋfɛstəv!] 節慶
Christmas is one of the most important **festivals** in America.
聖誕節是美國重要的節慶之一。

• **sponsor** (*v.*) [ˋspansɚ] 贊助
Could you tell me why we should **sponsor** the event?
你可以告訴我為什麼我們要贊助這活動嗎？

- **sponsorship** (*n.*) [`spɑnsɚʃɪp] 贊助
  The show is looking for **sponsorship** from those major banks.
  這場表演正在從那些大銀行那邊尋求贊助。

- **imagine** (*v.*) [ɪ`mædʒɪn] 想像
  Can you **imagine** what it's like when there's no wires?
  你能想像一個沒有電線的生活嗎?

- **lower** (*v.*) [`loɚ] 降低
  I don't think we should **lower** the price.
  我不認為我們應該降低價格。

- **exposure** (*n.*) [ɪk`spoʒɚ] 曝光;亮相
  Make sure the new product gets enough **exposure** this time.
  要確認這次新產品有足夠的曝光。

有料句型 Sentence Pattern

句型 1 ↘

Given that, ...　這樣的話,⋯。

Given that, how much is the cost of sponsorship for the items you mentioned?
這樣的話,請問一下您提到的贊助費用是需要多少呢?

Given that, I will call the photographer after the meeting.
這樣的話,會議結束後我會打個電話給攝影師。

Given that, there's a good chance that we will win this case this time.
這樣的話,我們這次贏這案子的機會很大。

1 行銷

2 廣告

3 媒體採購

4 公關公司

5 網路行銷

6 企業社會形象

句型 2 ↘

Please ... at your earliest convenience.　方便的話請儘速…。

Please also send me the contract **at your earliest convenience.**
方便的話請儘速一起將合約寄給我。

Please let me know when you will be available **at your earliest convenience.**
方便的話請儘速讓我知道您可以的時間。

Please give me a call **at your earliest convenience.**
方便的話請儘速打個電話給我。

Expert Tips
知識補給

Sponsorship is the material support to an event, activity or organization by an unrelated partner. It is a good way of increasing brand awareness, which helps to generate consumer preference and to foster brand loyalty.

贊助活動通常代表是由一個不完全相關的夥伴，對一個活動、表演或組織進行物品的資助，這是一個增加品牌曝光度的好方法，也可以幫助衍生消費者喜好度，與加強對品牌的忠誠度。

Dialogue 2　延伸對話 46

We Continue to Sponsor? 繼續贊助嗎？

☕ 情境說明 *Situation*

Linda is asking Jed if their company should sponsor sports competitions.

琳達正在針對公司是否應該贊助體育競賽活動請教杰德。

♀♂ 角色介紹 *Characters*

Linda: PR Account Executive
Jed: PR Manager

琳達：公關專員
杰德：公關經理

💬 情境對話 *Dialogue*

Linda: I am sorry to bother you, Jed.

琳達：杰德，抱歉打擾你一下。

Jed: Not a problem, what's up?

杰德：沒問題，請說。

Linda: About the competitions on road cycling Taiwan event, I think we should continue to sponsor. However, the required funds are so high, that's why I need to know your comments on it.

琳達：關於今年自行車環台的競賽活動，我想我們應該贊助。但是需求的款項都很高，所以我想請問你的看法。

1 行銷

2 廣告

3 媒體採購

4 公關公司

5 網路行銷

6 企業社會形象

Jed: The minimum amount is five hundred thousand, isn't it? Last year, we sponsored three hundred thousand.

杰德：最低是 50 萬元對吧？去年我們贊助了 30 萬元。

Linda: Yes, we did. So, what do you think of it? We continue to sponsor?

琳達：是的。怎麼樣？繼續贊助嗎？

Jed: What are those media exposures which are guaranteed by the organizer?

杰德：主辦單位保證的曝光程度有哪些呢？

Linda: In addittion to the exposures on TV, print media, they will host an evening dinner party which invited the President to join.

琳達：除了各大電視、平面媒體曝光外，還舉辦了晚宴，邀請了總統出席。

Jed: What a great chance, we can introduce our bicycle to the President by taking this opportunity!

杰德：機會難得，可以趁此契機向總統介紹我們公司的腳踏車呢！

短句補給 Useful Phrases

✓ I am sorry to bother you. 抱歉打擾你一下。

✓ I need to know your comments on it. 我想知道你對這件事的意見。

✓ We can introduce our product to... by taking this opportunity. 我們可以藉此向…介紹我們的商品。

品牌代言人
Brand Endorser

We have a pop star as our brand endorser. She is very popular and well known. I think that is why her agent is always having issues with how we use her visuals with our logo.

　　我們品牌使用一位流行演藝人員當代言人。她目前非常的受歡迎，知名度也很高。我想這也是她的經紀人，一直對我們的品牌標識如何搭配她的照片有很多意見的原因。

1 行銷

2 廣告

3 媒體採購

4 公關公司

5 網路行銷

6 企業社會形象

Dialogue 1　主題對話

We Need a Golden Team to Make Sure She Looks Great.
我們需要一個黃金團隊確保她看起來很棒。

情境說明 Situation

We are planning to use a visual of our brand endorser to make some POSMs (Point Of Sales Materials). Now the Product Manager is talking with the talent agent about visual shooting and usage.

我們正在安排使用幾張品牌代言人的視覺，來製作行銷製作物，目前產品經理正在與經紀人討論代言人視覺拍攝的細節與使用。

情境對話 Dialogue

Product Manager: The fitting date is November 10 and the shooting date is November 15.

產品經理：定裝日將在十一月十日，拍攝日則是十一月十五日。

Talent Agent: Please book the hairdresser Sunny from X Salon, make-up artist Beverly, and the stylist Ken on the shooting day. Our talent doesn't use any other hairdresser, make-up artist or stylist.

經紀人：請務必在拍攝日安排 X 沙龍的髮型設計師 Sunny，化妝師 Beverly 與造型師 Ken。我們的藝人不與其他任何髮型設計師、化妝師與造型師配合。

Product Manager: I see. But the cost for this hairdresser is a lot higher than those

產品經理：這樣啊。但是這一位髮型設計師的收取費

247

of other celebrities. Is she really necessary? We need just a simple horsetail.

用，比其他藝人的髮型設計師要高出很多，這位髮型設計師真的有必要嗎？因為我們只需要　一個簡單馬尾。

Talent Agent: Well, we want the golden team to ensure she looks good.

經紀人：這個嘛，我們要一個黃金團隊來保證藝人看起來很棒。

Product Manager: Fine. I will make sure they will be there on both fitting day and shooting day.

產品經理：好的，我會確定他們都會在定裝日與拍攝日出現。

Talent Agent: Good. Also, the visuals of our talent cannot be used in free giveaway POSMs. They must be printed out only on materials for those consumers who make purchases of a certain amount.

經紀人：很好，這些藝人的照片不能被使用在免費拿去或發送的製作物上，它們必須被印在一些製作物，讓消費者必須消費到特定金額才能得到的。

Product Manager: How about on the 2015 calendar?

產品經理：那麼如果是印在 2015 的月曆上？

Talent Agent: No. No numbers around the visual. To be clear, no numbers around her face.

經紀人：不可以，在藝人的視覺旁邊都不可以出現數字，我說清楚一點，她的臉部周邊不可以有數字。

1 行銷

2 廣告

3 媒體採購

4 公關公司

5 網路行銷

6 企業社會形象

Product Manager: How about on the back? We can print the calendar on the back and the front page would be her visual.

產品經理：那麼如果印在背面呢？我們可以將月曆印在視覺的背面，所以正面只會有她的視覺。

Talent Agent: How would you stitch each page? Any aperture surrounding the visual is not allowed.

經紀人：你會怎麼裝訂呢？任何裝訂孔出現在視覺旁邊也是不准的。

Product Manager: Not on the visual, but with a blank border?

產品經理：不是在視覺上，如果我們留一個白邊呢？

Talent Agent: No way. I don't like the idea of a calendar at all. Please also do not print the visual onto a mug, poster or notebook. I have listed those items on the contract as "not allowed to be produced."

經紀人：不可以，我不喜歡這個製作月曆的想法，請不要印任何我們家藝人的照片在馬克杯、海報、或筆記本。我當初有將這些項目寫在合約上，這些都是不被准許製作的。

ABC 有料字彙 Vocabulary

- **endorser** (*n.*) [ɪn`dɔrsɚ] 背書人　brand endorser 品牌代言人
  Brand **endorsers** influence sales volume directly.
  品牌代言人直接影響著銷售量。

- **fitting** (*n.*) [`fɪtɪŋ] 試穿，試衣
  She will come next Monday for a **fitting**.
  她下週一會來試衣。

- **hairdresser** (*n.*) [`hɛr͵drɛsɚ] 美髮師
  I have been going to my **hairdresser**, Jenny for years.
  我已經在美髮師珍妮那邊（弄頭髮）好幾年了。

- **make-up** (*n.*) [`mek͵ʌp] 化妝；裝扮；化妝品
  She put up some **make-up** for the speech.
  她為了這場化了點妝。

- **stylist** (*n.*) [`staɪlɪst] 造型師
  Alan was the top **stylist** at the salon.
  亞倫是那家沙龍的首席設計師。

- **horsetail** (*n.*) [`hɔrs͵tel] 馬尾
  Let me show you how to DIY a trendy **horsetail** hairstyle.
  讓我來示範如何自己綁個時髦的馬尾髮型給你看。

- **giveaway** (*n.*) [`gɪvə͵we] 贈送的（贈品）
  The **giveaway** of the day is worth looking forward to.
  「今日贈品」很值得期待。

- **stitch** (*v.*) [stɪtʃ]（縫線的）一針；裝訂
  We **stitched** those pages back together to the traditional pattern.
  我們把那些書頁裝訂回傳統的樣式。

- **aperture** (*n.*) [ˈæpətʃə] 孔徑；裝訂孔
The ribbons passed through **apertures** in the ceiling.
緞帶穿過天花板的小孔。

- **border** (*n.*) [ˈbɔrdə] 邊緣；邊沿
You need a piece of paper with black **border**.
你需要一張邊緣是黑色的紙。

有料句型 Sentence Pattern

句型 1 ↘

We want the golden team to...　我們要這黃金團隊去…。

We want the golden team to ensure she looks good.
我們要這黃金團隊來確保她看起來很棒。

We want the golden team to create all the glamour.
我們要這黃金團隊來創造這所有的魅力。

We want the golden team to make this happen.
我們要這黃金團隊來把這實現。

句型 2 ↘

I will make sure...　我會確保…（一定會做好）。

I will make sure they will be there on both fitting day and shooting day.
我會確定他們都會在定裝日與拍攝日出現。

I will make sure everything goes and nothing matters.
我會確保一切都順利不會有事的。

I will make sure he gets your massage.
我會確保他收到您的留言的。

Expert Tips
知識補給

There are a number of advantages to using celebrities in advertising such as attracting new users, building awareness, influencing consumer behavior, and positioning the brand. However, you have to be careful selecting the celebrity that suits your brand and uses your products. Also, careful about the contract content; some details could really impact day-to-day work.

使用一位名人代言有很多的好處與品牌優勢，比如説吸引新的消費者、品牌知名度建立、影響消費行為，甚至是加強品牌定位，但是名人也是要慎選，不但要挑適合自己品牌形象，且也是該產品愛用者。另外，在合約的內容上要很小心，有些細節是大大影響到一般的工作內容。

1 行銷

2 廣告

3 媒體採購

4 公關公司

5 網路行銷

6 企業社會形象

Dialogue 2　延伸對話 48

Choose A Brand Ambassador. 選擇品牌大使

 情境說明 *Situation*

Ryan and Kimberly are eating lunch together at staff dining room, and they are talking about what kind of celebrity should be hired to be the brand ambassador.

雷恩與金柏莉一起在員工餐廳用午餐，他們正聊起了應該請哪一種明星擔任公司的品牌代言人。

♀♂ **角色介紹** *Characters*

Ryan: Advertising Account Executive
Kimberly: PR Account Executive

雷恩：廣告部專員
金柏莉：公關專員

 情境對話 *Dialogue*

Ryan: Kimberly, come and join me. Wow, you eat really light.

雷恩：金柏莉，歡迎與我同桌。哇，妳吃得好清淡喔。

Kimberly: I had diarrhea this morning.

金柏莉：我早上拉肚子了呢。

Ryan: I see. Right, have you heard of that? The company wants us to select a brand

雷恩：原來如此。對了，妳聽說了嗎？公司希望我們票

ambassador.

選出品牌代言人。

Kimberly: So I have been told. What a wise decision. Our past brand ambassador is totally lack of stringency.

金柏莉：聽説了。真是一個明智的決定。之前我們的代言人一點兒説服力也沒有。

Ryan: What's in your mind?

雷恩：妳有何高見？

Kimberly: I think we need a sporty or manly one.

金柏莉：我覺得要找一個運動型或者很有男子氣概的代言人。

Ryan: I would rather choose a sunshine boy to express the fresh feeling after finishing our energy drink.

雷恩：我倒覺得陽光型男比較符合我們飲料，喝完後感到神清氣爽的那種感覺。

Kimberly: Oh yah? Whatever. By the way, you haven't bought me a meal yet.

金柏莉：是嗎？隨你喜歡。對了，你還少請我吃一頓飯呢。

Ryan: Sorry, I forgot it. I'll make it up to you someday.

雷恩：抱歉，我忘了。改天我會補償妳的啦。

🐨 短句補給 Useful Phrases

✓ I bad diarrhea this morning. 我今天早上拉肚子了。
✓ It is totally lack of stringency. 這完全沒有説服力。
✓ I'll make it up to you someday. 改天我會補償你的。

N o t e s

慈善活動
Charity Projects

Corporate philanthropy is an import subject to us. Not only because it can help the company save on taxes, but also because it can enhance the company's reputation.

企業慈善活動對我們而言，是一個重要的議題，不只是因為可以幫助品牌節稅，也是因為這是一個很好的機會，提升公司的聲譽。

1 行銷

2 廣告

3 媒體採購

4 公關公司

5 網路行銷

6 企業社會形象

Dialogue 1　主題對話

Those Previous Photos Did Not Look Good Or Attract Media Attention. 過去那些照片不是很上相，也不夠吸引媒體注意。

情境說明 *Situation*

Our team is having a meeting to discuss what topic should be next year's corporate philanthropy target.

我們團隊正在開會，討論明年度企業慈善活動的主題與目標。

情境對話 *Dialogue*

Marketing Manager: The company's Corporate Philanthropy Guidelines indicate that corporate philanthropy should involve only two areas, which are elderly care and disaster relief.

行銷經理：在公司的企業慈善活動準則裡面，指出只能介入兩個主要的慈善範圍，第一個是老人照護，另一個是災難救助。

PR Manager: Yes, but it is not every day that we have a disaster. Therefore, basically, we are planning to focus on elderly care.

公關經理：是的，而災難救助也並不是時常會有機會發生，因此我們想著重在老人照護的方向。

Marketing Manager: I know. But those previous elderly care photos did not look good or attract media attention.

行銷經理：我懂，不過，過去那些老人照護活動的照片，都不是很上相，也不夠吸引媒體的目光與報導興趣。

257

PR Manager: Well, the old people we have been trying to help are usually sick or disabled. They don't look pretty like models — that is for sure.

公關經理：這個嘛，那些我們過去幫助的老人都是有病症的，或是殘障人士，因此他們當然不會像模特兒一般上相好看，這是當然的。

Marketing Manager: How can we overcome this barrier. We have to make our elderly care efforts look nice so more media will report on what we are doing and so enhance company awareness and reputation.

行銷經理：我們要如何克服這個障礙。我們要讓我們對老人照護的努力，在媒體與攝影鏡頭前是美觀的，因此才會有較多的媒體進行報導，公司所進行的企業慈善活動，藉以提高公司的知名度與聲譽。

PR Manager: I am thinking we could conduct an "elderly dream comes true" campaign. We interview 20 better-looking elderly people and see what their dreams were when they were younger. We help them to accomplish their dreams now and make a book and also a photo exhibition afterward. That could raise not only media interest, but also the public's interest.

公關經理：我一直在想，我們可以企劃一個「夢想不老，願望成真」的活動，我們訪問二十位較上相的老人，並看看他們年輕時的願望是什麼，我們幫助他們實現願望，並將故事集結成書，未來還可以辦一場攝影展，這一定可以引起媒體的專注，不只如此，還可以引起大眾的關注。

Marketing Manager: That is a really good idea.

行銷經理：這真的是一個很棒的想法。

1 行銷
2 廣告
3 媒體採購
4 公關公司
5 網路行銷
6 企業社會形象

PR Manager: I am also thinking we could share the old people's smiling faces and happy looks with the media along with stories of their achievements. It's much more convincing and interesting than just telling the media what our company has done.

公關經理：我還在想，分享這些老人的笑臉與開心快樂的表情，搭配上願望成真的故事，比單單告訴媒體我們做了什麼慈善活動，來得更有說服力與有趣的多。

Marketing Manager: I agree. Let's do that next year!

行銷經理：我同意，我們就明年開始吧！

PR Manager: I will have to find an elderly nursing home that is willing to co-operate with us, and that has a good reputation.

公關經理：我要先找一個願意與我們配合的老人安養機構，並且這個機構也得要有好的聲譽才行。

Marketing Manager: Right. Association XXX in Taiwan had a financial scandal recently. We have to be cautious with our selection.

行銷經理：沒錯，近來台灣的 XXX 機構發生了一些財務糾紛醜聞，我們必須要小心這些合作單位的選擇。

ABC 有料字彙 Vocabulary

- **philanthropy** (*n.*) [fɪˋlænθrəpɪ] 仁慈；慈善事業
  The company devotes large-scale resources to nonprofit organizations and **philanthropy.**
  這家公司貢獻了龐大的資源在非營利組織和慈善事業。

- **elderly** (*adj.*) [ˋɛldəlɪ] 年長的；上了年紀的
  The product is designed for the **elderly**.
  這產品是為了上了年紀的人設計的。

- **disaster** (*n.*) [dɪˋzæstə] 災害；災難
  The agreement turned out to be the greatest **disaster** in the foreign policy.
  結果這協議變成外交政策上最大的災難。

- **disable** (*v.*) [dɪsˋeb!] 使失去能力
  Hackers threaten to **disable** their websites unless money is paid.

- **overcome** (*v.*) [͵ovəˋkʌm] 戰勝；克服
  A better preparation cannot **overcome** the bad initial impression.
  更充份的準備也無法克服不好的初次印象。

- **barrier** (*n.*) [ˋbærɪr] 障礙物
  They overcame the language **barrier** in the end and succeeded in overseas market.
  他們最後克服了語言障礙，在海外市場獲得成功。

- **convincing** (*adj.*) [kənˋvɪnsɪŋ] 有說服力的
  The story was brief but **convincing**.
  這故事雖簡短但是有說服力。

- **nursing** (*adj.*) [ˋnɝsɪŋ] 看護；養育　nursing home 療養院
  She needs twenty-four-hour nursing care for months.
  她有好幾個月需要二十四小時的看護。

- **scandal** (*n.*) [ˋskænd!] 醜聞，可恥的事
  It is a **scandal** for government officials to take bribes.
  政府官員收受賄賂是件醜聞（可恥的事）

- **cautious** (*adj.*) [ˋkɔʃəs] 小心謹慎的
  You should be more **cautious** about making promises.
  你應該更小心謹慎做出承諾。

🐦🐦 有料句型 *Sentence Pattern*

句型 1 ↘

Those previous... did not... 這些之前的⋯並不⋯。

Those previous elderly care photos **did not** look good or attract media attention.
過去那些老人照護活動的照片，都不是很上相，也不夠吸引媒體目光與報導興趣。

Those previous commercials **were not** strikingly successful.
這些之前的廣告並沒有十分地成功。

Those previous catalogues **didn't** feature the touch screen monitor.
這些之前的目錄並沒有標榜觸控螢幕的特色。

句型 2 ↘

It is not every day that... ⋯不是每天都有的事。

It is not every day that we have a disaster.
災難大也並不是時常會有機會發生。

It is not every day that you see an outstanding proposal.
一份傑出的提案不是每天都有的事。

It is not every day that you find someone you can put up with.
找到那個你可以忍受的人可不是每天都有的事。

1 行銷

2 廣告

3 媒體採購

4 公關公司

5 網路行銷

6 企業社會形象

Expert Tips
知識補給

Doing corporate philanthropy means bridging and aligning the company's goals and nonprofit missions. It's not just the right thing to do; it's also crucial to both business and culture. Some companies encourage employees to join and be involved with these non-profitable activities. As for the outcome, the key is to have effective partnerships.

進行企業慈善活動可以為公司的目標與非營利單位的目標，建立起一個合作的橋樑，這不只是做對的事，對文化影響與企業經營也相對重要，有些企業還會鼓勵員工去參加這些非營利單位的活動，至於結果，還是關乎於與這些單位的有效率之合作關係。

Dialogue 2　延伸對話

The Originally Planned Celebrity on the A-List Cannot Come.
原定的 A 咖藝人不能來了。

 情境說明 *Situation*

Evelyn and Kristen are discussing how to plan the Company's year-end charity sponsorship event.

伊芙琳與克莉絲坦正在商量該如何策劃公司的年末慈善贊助活動。

♀♂ **角色介紹** *Characters*

Evelyn: PR Account Executive
Kristen: PR Manager

伊芙琳：公關專員
克莉絲坦：公關經理

💬 **情境對話** *Dialogue*

Evelyn: Kristen, I feel I have my luck run out.

伊芙琳：克莉絲坦，我覺得我運氣用光了。

Kristen: What's going on?

克莉絲坦：怎麼了？

Evelyn: It's the year-end charity sponsorship event, the originally planned A-list celebrity cannot come.

伊芙琳：是年末的慈善贊助活動，原定的 A 咖藝人不能來了。

1 行銷

2 廣告

3 媒體採購

4 公關公司

5 網路行銷

6 企業社會形象

Kristen: Then we have to hire one on the B-list. Remember, don't hire a comedian or an entertainer.

克莉絲坦：那只好請 B 咖級的了。記住，不要找搞笑藝人或綜藝咖。

Evelyn: Sure. By the way, one of the donees refused to accept the donations.

伊芙琳：知道。另外，受贈的單位竟然有一家拒絕接受捐款。

Kristen: I see, I start to have a bad feeling about this as well. Well, we can only look for another donation receivers.

克莉絲坦：這樣啊，我也開始有不好的預感了。只好另尋其他受贈單位了。

Evelyn: I also want to confirm with you that if the mascot can continue on the stage for one hour?

伊芙琳：我還想確定一下，品牌吉祥物當天是不是可以連續出場 1 小時？

Kristen: No, he cannot, because the part-time employee needs to take some rest. Is that all?

克莉絲坦：不行，吉祥物裡面的工讀生需要休息。就是這些了吧？

Evelyn: Yes. No matter how difficult it is, things still need to get done, don't they?

伊芙琳：是的。不管再怎麼辛苦，事情還是要做的，對吧。

短句補給 Useful Phrases

✓ I feel I have my luck ran out. 我覺得我運氣用光了。

✓ The originally planned person cannot come. 原定的人不能來。

✓ I start to have a bad feeling about this. 我開始有不好的預感。

好書報報 –生活系列

BEST BOOKS
Best Publishing

愛情之酒甜而苦。兩人喝，是甘露；
三人喝，是酸醋；隨便喝，要中毒。

精選出偶像劇必定出現的**8o**個情境，
每個情境－必備單字、劇情會話訓練班、30秒會話教室
讓你跟著偶像劇的腳步學生活英語會話的劇情，
輕鬆自然地學會英語!

作者：伍羚芝
定價：新台幣349元
規格：344頁 / 18K / 雙色印刷

全書中英對照，介紹東西方節慶的典故，
幫助你的英語學習－學得好、學得深入!

用英語來學節慶分為兩大部分－東方節慶&西方節慶

每個節慶共**7**個學習項目：
節慶源由－簡易版、精彩完整版＋實用單字、閱讀測驗、
習俗放大鏡、實用會話、常用單句這麼說、互動單元...

作者：Melanie Venekamp、陳欣慧、倍斯特編輯團隊
定價：新台幣299元
規格：304頁 / 18K / 雙色印刷

用現有的環境與資源，為自己的小寶貝
創造一個雙語學習環境；讓孩子贏在起跑點上!

我家寶貝愛英文，是一本從媽咪懷孕、嬰兒期到幼兒期，
會常用到的單字、對話，必備例句，
並設計單元延伸的互動小遊戲以及童謠，
增進親子關係，也讓家長與孩子一同學習的參考書!

作者：Mark Venekamp & Claire Chang
定價：新台幣329元
規格：296頁 / 18K / 雙色印刷 / MP3

Leader 002

行銷公關英語超有料(MP3)
Charming & Glowing: Communications in Marketing, Advertising and PR

作　　者　　江昀璟　胥淑嵐
發 行 人　　周瑞德
企劃執行　　劉俞青
封面設計　　高鍾琪
內文排版　　菩薩蠻數位文化有限公司
校　　對　　徐瑞璞　陳欣慧

印　　製　　世和印製企業有限公司
初　　版　　2014 年 8 月
出　　版　　力得文化
電　　話　　（02）2351-2007
傳　　真　　（02）2351-0887
地　　址　　100 台北市中正區福州街 1 號 10 樓之 2
Ｅｍａｉｌ　　best.books.service@gmail.com
定　　價　　新台幣 329 元

港澳地區總經銷　　　泛華發行代理有限公司
地　　　　址　　　香港筲箕灣東旺道 3 號星島新聞集團大廈 3 樓
電　　　　話　　　（852）2798-2323
傳　　　　真　　　（852）2796-5471

國家圖書館出版品預行編目(CIP)資料

行銷公關英語超有料 / 江昀璟　胥淑嵐著 ── 初版.
── 臺北市： 力得文化, 2014.08
　　面；　公分. ──（Leader；2）
　ISBN 978-986-90759-1-6（平裝附光碟片）

　1. 英語 2. 職場 3. 會話

805.188　　　　　　　　　　　　103013578

力得文化
Leader Culture

Lead your way, be your own leader!

力得文化
Leader Culture

Lead your way, be your own leader!